D0007614

the blessing
and the curse

THE JEWISH PUBLICATION SOCIETY
1888-1988

the blessing & the curse

LINDA BAYER

THE JEWISH PUBLICATION SOCIETY
Philadelphia New York Jerusalem 5748—1988

Copyright © 1988 by Linda Bayer
First edition All rights reserved
Manufactured in the United States of America

Library of Congress Cataloging in Publication Data
Bayer, Linda.
The blessing and the curse.
I. Title.
PS3552.A8587B57 1988 813'.54 87–33881
ISBN 0–8276–0309–6

The characters in this novel are entirely fictitious. Specifically, no faculty or students from Boston University, American University, Wesleyan University, the Hartford College for Women, the University of New Haven, Clark University, the Hebrew University, New York University, Colby-Sawyer College, Florida State University, or Harvard University have been depicted. Any resemblance to real people should be considered coincidental.

to Ilana and Lev

part one

1

Ladies and gentlemen, the captain has turned on the no-smoking sign, and we have begun our descent into Boston. Please be sure your seat belts are securely fastened and your tray tables are locked in the upright position for landing. The temperature in Boston is a balmy eighty-seven degrees with partly overcast skies. We may encounter some turbulence at the lower altitudes, and we therefore ask that you remain in your seats. We hope you have enjoyed your flight and thank you for choosing USAir.

If only the plane could stay up a little longer, suspended between blue absence and a green checkerboard—perfect fields with neat edges, so orderly from a distance. Like a coloring book.

"Yes, thank you. I didn't realize we were landing already." Ida fastened the catch on her tray table.

For the last half hour they had been circling in a holding pattern. Above crooked rivers and looped highways, crossed obliquely by the passing thought of a lower plane. On the seat beside Ida lay her curriculum vita and a copy of the book she had written: *Women Poets of the Nineteenth Century*. The jacket was slipping off. From the flyleaf a picture of the author stared back at Ida like a stranger.

Ida flipped through one of her course outlines. "The Absurd in the Arts." She tried to remember the plays she had taught. *The Rhinoceros*, not *The Hippopotamus*. And Arp painted *Mountains Table Anchors Navel*. Arp. Don't forget Arp. Ida wondered if she had time to reread the chapter she'd written on the symbolic use of flowers in romantic verse.

Manchester, not Hartford. Even in the sixth grade she'd still gotten it wrong in the underlined blank for her birthplace. Once, on the phone, she even lost her name! For one panicky moment. Ida detested interviews. With her head against the window, the panorama blurred to aqua as she stared at the empty space between the inner and outer panes of glass.

> Welcome to Boston. For your own safety and comfort, we request that you remain in your seats until the aircraft has taxied into the gate and come to a complete stop. Please be sure to remove any valuables you may have brought on board with you.

The ceiling of the plane, with its bony ridges and recesses, looked like the skeleton of a great fish that had swallowed a school of minnows. Ida had always liked small places. Snug, not cramped. Like the space where she used to crouch under her father's bushel baskets—with the smell of warm tomato plants and her own hands.

She rhythmically snapped the top of the safety belt without unlatching it. Arp. Manchester. *The Rhinoceros*. Flowers stand for fragility. Beauty that is temporal, seasonal. Female periodicity. Arp. *The Rhinoceros*. Arp. *The Rhinoceros*. Reluctantly, Ida stepped out into the flow of dark suits and flowered prints moving through the belly of the plane.

Checking her watch: 9:10. Another hour and twenty minutes until her appointment at the University.

GROUND TRANSPORTATION—LOWER LEVEL. At the bottom of the escalator the automatic doors opened for her, and she crossed the shaded street beneath the airport overpass to the bus. *33 to the T, then the blue line to the green line*. Ida reviewed the underlined instructions she'd copied yesterday onto a note card placed in the front of her manila folder. *Take the Boston College car*. Her new shoes pinched at the heels. Low pumps. "Watch your step, Ma'am." Tokens may be purchased inside. *Change trains at Government Center*.

Between stops the subway was dark. Sitting close to her wide-eyed reflection in the window, Ida was roughly rocked back and forth as the subway charged beneath the city. Park, Boylston, Arlington, Copley, Auditorium. 9:45. Still plenty of time. Ida reread the advertisement for a professorship in the humanities that she'd clipped from the *Chronicle of Higher Education* last February. Why had they waited till August to set up interviews?

After Kenmore Station the train headed upward into the light. Into dormitory towers on top of storefronts and flat, gray masonry, tickled here and there by a Gothic carving. An occasional giggle on a granite roar. Ida remembered the student union where she used to meet Rob. Always here, never at Brandeis. Too much green on your campus, he used to say. All that green rots the brain. Come on into the city, Ida. I'll meet you in front of the B.U. union.

B.U. Be me. We're one. Be free. The senseless mantra Ida had repeated to herself on so many trips to visit Rob. After her last class, before his vacation, during exam week. All those long ago visits to Rob.

At the crest of the hill the train paused for traffic over the bridge. Ida got out at the following stop.

DIVISION OF GENERAL EDUCATION. Gold letters on a framed sign marked the entrance, but Ida walked past it toward the School of Fine Arts. She didn't want to be seen half an hour early. Ten minutes would be acceptable. In the meantime, there was the ladies' room, with its mirror and low seat and locked door.

Ida stared at the toilet paper roll and the space beneath the door. She counted the symmetrical tiles on the floor. By twos, by fives. Then she straightened her hair, tightening the clip in the back. Arp. *The Rhinoceros*. Three years of college teaching. The first at Colby College for Women. Where Charlie Bolster, in the philosophy department, was hired instead of an attractive woman because the faculty wives didn't want their husbands working "with a lady who looked like *that*." Ida buttoned the top of her blouse.

In the student lounge she bought a Coke and slowly drank it while rereading the plaudits on the back of her book. Intellectually exciting, fresh style, comprehensive. Ida straightened her skirt. Enough already. Too much. She headed for the office they'd told her to find. Room 201 in the adjacent building. 201. 201. Rethink, reread, review, rehearse. The dreaded *re* disease. Ida hated interviews.

Before she could reach the second floor, a young man intercepted her. His black hair was a little too long. To the edge of his collar. He had been reading near the doorway on a bench against the wall. He stood as she approached.

"Are you Dr. Weiss?"

"Yes. Ida." She extended her hand. "So *you're* early too." His fingers bunched in hers. Like a clump of celery sticks.

"Nice to meet you. I'm Tom Martin. The committee convened half an hour ago to review your application—they're ready for you in the conference room." Climbing the stairs with Ida, he bounced his rolled newspaper off alternate rungs of the banister. "They're actually a nice group of people. Mast's a bit stiff, Steigler's somewhat disoriented, and Harrington is a prince. Don't pay any attention if he's a little aggressive. Or pompous. By the way, they're quite impressed with you already."

As though they were on the same side of the net. Group interviews were like trying to volley against an entire team. "Thank you. I'm glad to be here."

"We really must apologize for hiring so late. You see, first we thought a colleague would be leaving for medical reasons, but later his situation changed. Then, less than a month ago, another member of the department accepted a job in Colorado, so we simply reactivated the earlier applications. Tell me, if I'm not being nosy, how could you leave your present post with so little notice?"

Pausing on the landing between the flights of stairs. "I'm on sabbatical this fall, so if I did change jobs, Georgetown would have plenty of time to look for my replacement."

During the interview, Ida sat at the head of an oval table. Tom Martin was at the far end, pencil in hand. He seemed to be drawing pictures of the other faculty members. Mast conducted the meeting. "The Division of General Education is a two-year honors program at Boston University. Our students must apply separately to D.G.E.; we accept less than half of the applicants. Hence we deal with an elite group drawn to an interdisciplinary curriculum. That's why your own background, in both the literature and art of the Romantic period, made you particularly attractive to us."

There was one woman on the committee. Stocky, with no neck. "Dr. Weiss, I had a question about *your* interest in our position. Incidentally, do you prefer to be called Morgan-Weiss or just Weiss?"

A question of identity or politics? Feminism or etiquette? "I publish under my full name, but the hyphen is cumbersome. So I often use just Weiss—I did for years, as you can see from my earlier articles—and once in a while I use Morgan. Why don't you call me Ida?"

"Ida, why do you want to leave your present job? I notice from your vita that you've taught at quite a number of different colleges."

A backhand shot. Should she allude to personal reasons? Unprofessional. But otherwise they'd wonder about conflicts at work. Or mental illness, or legal entanglements. Recently separated from her husband? Sounds like emotional problems. "Over the years I've alternately taught in English and art history departments. My academic career sometimes reminds me of those sinks with separate faucets for hot and cold water—you move your hands from one to the other to achieve the right temperature. Your program offers the opportunity of combining the verbal and the visual, using each to enhance the other."

At the end of the table Tom Martin looked up for the first time. He swallowed a smile. And began to sketch bathroom equipment.

The man who had been introduced as William Harrington cleared his throat. "You understand, of course, that as a two-year program we don't offer upper-level seminars on special topics. Scholarly pursuits can atrophy here, cut off from graduate students to share in research. Some people consider our courses introductory surveys with insufficient depth. How would you react to such an assessment?" A well-placed serve.

"I've taught graduate seminars as well as freshman courses, as you can see from my résumé, and I do enjoy the challenge of more advanced work, but there's a special thrill to beginnings, to helping students discover the language of art when they first realize that it's about the mind as well as the eye. Maybe I'm drawn to virginity—to sharing in what's fresh, unpracticed."

"An occupational hazard of the nineteenth century?" Mast wagged his head like a puppy.

"I suppose so. Anyway, I guess when the distance between me and the students is greater, as it is with underclassmen, the challenge to bridge is greater—the need to reach. The rewards are greater, too. Anyway, I find nothing superficial about studying selections by twenty great writers as opposed to all the works of a single author."

"But the amount of *time* you can devote is restricted. I sometimes feel I can never scratch the surface because we're so devoted to the overview." Harrington tapped the end of his pen. A fountain pen. The old kind where the point separates after a while and makes two lines. When you bear down.

"How can I put it? A telescope doesn't show you any more or less than a microscope; the issue is simply to choose the proper focus for the distance. You can't learn topography from cells or molecular structure from aerial maps. I don't mind the overview as long as I can land here and there to give the students a closer look."

"How high do you fly?" Martin didn't look up.

"It doesn't matter, as long as the lens matches the altitude."

The interview lasted over an hour, after which Ida was given a tour of the classrooms and lecture halls. She asked about scheduling and the yearly calendar, book orders, and class size. Mast spoke further of the late hiring date, citing inaccurate enrollment projections, the budgetary freeze, and glacial bureaucratic procedures compounded by unforeseen personal changes. Ida was the last of three candidates.

She was impatient to leave. Like an actor following a performance, she felt uncomfortable socializing in the theater. With the audience. Backstage she could linger with the character she had created. An understudy cast in her own image.

When she asked to use a phone, Mast unlocked a vacant office on the third floor. He mentioned some misadventures with a faulty transmission and finally hurried off to join his wife at a service station before his afternoon meetings. "Just slam the door behind you when you're finished."

Some flight confirmations and a call to her cousin in Waltham before she slumped back in the swivel chair. On wheels. Gliding along the waxed floor with its unscuffed summer look. Shining like intermission at the Ice Capades, when the buffer machine licks the ice to glass. Her feet off the floor, Ida pushed back from the desk and spun around in the chair. She filled the silent room with a sliding sound—a cross between a sigh and a cheer.

"It went that well, did it?"

A blur of corduroy in the spinning doorway. Ida grabbed the desk corner as it slid by, the arm of her chair crashing into the open top drawer. "Well, for an encore I was practicing my gyroscope imitation." She groped with bare feet for her shoes. "I always wind up like this, you see. But usually not in public. I thought I was alone."

"Sorry to surprise you like that. I was working in the next office with the door closed. Generally there's no one here in the summer. The name's Phil Manning, sociology."

"Nice to meet you. I'm Ida Morgan-Weiss."

Manning stepped into the office and leaned against the bookcase. He moved with the athletic ease of the thinner man he must have been twenty years ago. Large hands hung from his wrists as though waiting for his arms to grow. Like on the *David,* Ida thought. The hand that barely closed around the stone.

"So, you think you got the job." He cocked his head and looked to the side of the chair. Ida's white slip was folded over her pocketbook. She nudged it under the desk with her foot. Manning started to laugh. "Really, I am sorry."

Ida steadied one wrist against her lap, trying to hook her watchband. "It's awfully hot today. Sweaty and . . . the leather strap . . ."

"The job's yours, you think?"

"No, that depends on the other candidates. I just feel that I gave a good interview."

"And what's a good interview?"

Ida stared at the picture hangers painted tan with the rest of the room. "When you don't make any mistakes, of course, and you're, well, all of a piece—all in the same style. Articulate, pleasant, intelligent—right? Yet manage to show yourself a little. A good interview has a slow leak."

"What would you want to show them?"

Bracing her foot against the desk, Ida rolled the chair

back on its casters. "That I can get a little closer to the works, and to the students. Help the kids make the poems theirs. We all know the tools of the trade, we can all teach woodworking, so to speak, but I can bring the statue to life for students." Like Pinocchio, she reflected. This sounds ridiculous. "That beyond the fear there is a flair."

"You couldn't mask the fear, then."

She noticed the lines around his eyes, chiseled too deeply as though for viewing from afar. "Not entirely."

"Flair, beauty, and honesty too. And I really liked the spinning. Hope you get the job, Morgan-Weiss."

In retrospect, Ida considered the plane imagery she'd used in the interview. Flighty. They're probably thinking they don't need a pilot, or a stewardess. Or a doll with a wooden head. Had the interview gone well, after all? She pictured the other candidates—composed, reserved. Speaking of genre, nuance, and narrative voice. The critical spectrum and contemporary verse, not hot and cold running water.

"Yes, Mother, the interview went well. I had a nice day with Marsha afterwards, and we both stayed overnight with her friend in Brookline. Marsha's an early riser, so she drove me to the airport."

"Sure, it's Delta Flight 423 landing at Bradley at 8:22. I'm sorry it's so early, but this way we'll have plenty of time to get to services."

"Absolutely not. If you cancel your flight to Houston on Monday, I won't come at all. We have two days together now plus the holidays next weekend. Really, I'm fine, and Pearl's counting on you. You've been looking forward to a week with your grandson all summer."

"Mom, I saw the baby in May at the *bris*, and I just can't spare the time. If I do get the job, I have so many things to close out in Washington, and classes begin September twelfth. Listen, we'll talk when I see you. This is ridiculous."

"Yes, thank you. I put the flight on your credit card. And Mom, please, relax. I'm all right. See you in an hour. Bye."

> This is the final boarding call for Flight 423 to Hartford. All remaining passengers should report immediately to gate 26.

A clear Saturday morning. From her window seat Ida watched the plane ahead of hers taxi down the runway and ease into the sky, a stream billowing out behind it like

Elmer's glue on a blue background. Ida thought of a collage she'd made for Rob from glossy photos of the places they'd lived. A present for his thirtieth birthday. Pasted together on posterboard. Trimmed snapshots—Rose in Paris, Passover with Aunt Grace, the house in Seattle—all scattered across the blue matting. Linked by silver wings and white exhaust. Don't use Elmer's glue with photographs—the instructions on the front of the paste jar. But the pictures weren't ruined. Wedding shots and beach scenes, camping in the Rockies. Rob's girlfriend wouldn't want it in her living room. So Ida would keep the collage.

Before she realized, her plane was in the air. Outside the window, the wings were dwarfed by single clouds. Silent splendor. Ida recalled the lines in the Sabbath service, "*Kadosh, kadosh, kadosh, Adonai tzevaot.*" The congregation would rise three times on tiptoes. A gesture toward the heights. "Holy, holy, holy is the Lord of hosts." The Lord of reverent cumulus clouds.

When the plane began to land, she swallowed repeatedly to ease the pressure in her ears. Ida had not seen her mother since she and Rob separated in May. She'd avoided Manchester, the only place left where people didn't move away. Where horse chestnuts grew in prickly pods, slippery smooth on the inside, and the ice froze early on Charter Oak pond. For skating. Gray-green up close, the color of mica. Thin strips to peel off the sides of rocks and keep in white cardboard boxes with cotton pads on the bottom. "Keep those boxes out of the living room, Ida. Put them away in the bedroom. With your bird egg collection." Her mother's eyes were hazel, like the mica and the ice on the pond. You could see yourself in her glasses when the light was just right.

Ida dreaded this visit. Like bringing home a broken gift.

"Ida always brings me the nicest presents." Baskets of woven construction paper filled with crayoned flowers, and light blue report cards with at least three A's. Glowing letters from Paris and xeroxed reviews of her book. Ida remembered the Buckley School talent show, the auditorium filled with mothers, where she had won second prize for playing the piano. "Clair de Lune." Her friend Bonnie Ralston recited a poem but in the middle forgot the lines. After leaving the stage in tears, Bonnie kept repeating how glad she was that her mother could not attend.

Mildred Morgan bought a second cup of instant coffee from the vending machine. At four o'clock that morning she had stopped trying to fall asleep and began cleaning the odds-and-ends drawer next to the refrigerator. Then she oiled the cherrywood tables in the den and baked a coffee cake for Ida to take home. Cinnamon bobka, with extra raisins. The crusty ones on the top burned. She'd arrived at the airport half an hour early after running out of house projects. But the plane was slightly delayed. A longer wait. Finally she sighted her daughter walking alone toward the end of the deplaning crowd.

"Darling, I'm so happy to see you. To be together for Dad's *Yahrzeit*, especially this year. You look fine, Ida. When did you get that skirt?"

"Hi, Mom." Through the fishbowl of her mother's thick glasses: watery eyes. Enlarged. Ida looked away from them and fought to steady her own voice. In the car, belted into the gold upholstery, she felt better. Heavier. Against her bare arms the cushion rubbed like the fur on a new teddy bear. Her mother's spotless car never lost that just-bought smell. They talked for a while about Aunt Grace's polyps, Pearl's new baby, and the job at Boston University. At the traffic circle near Bower School, Mildred drove around twice.

"Ida dear, it all happened so suddenly. I just don't understand. Rob—you mean he just fell out of love? But he always seemed so . . ."

"Love isn't something you're *in*, Mother. Like labor, or a bathtub."

"Ida, before you get so flip . . ."

"Anyway, that has nothing to do with it. Rob still loves me. He just loves her too."

Mildred pulled over to the side of the road for the red Caprice that had been tailing her. It passed noisily. "But if you love someone . . . well, I've always thought that if there's another woman it means that the wife—that is, at least there's something wrong with the marriage or . . ."

"Mother, you don't know anything about this."

"Now Ida, I don't understand why you're always so quick to . . ."

"Mom, Rob saw other women from the start. Socially. He detested the idea of *having* a wife, of owning one like a possession. He felt that way before he even met me. So when he got to know Sheila and things grew between them, well, that was it."

"I just think that if you look into your own heart—Ida, stop that. You'll ruin your hair if you keep pulling on it . . . I was saying, maybe he'd get tired of her, or that other woman would get tired, if you just . . ."

"It's been going on for two years now, Mom. I never said anything to you before because . . . well, what would be the point? It would only upset you. But now, I can't wait any more for him. First it was waiting for children—for him to want them—and now this. He was perfectly willing to . . . but it kept eroding. We wanted different things, that's all."

The car stalled at the corner of Parker and Green. "That alternator. I don't know why they can't fix it! I keep bringing the car in, and they say it's fine every time." Mildred pumped the gas until the engine whined in protest. "Anyway, Ida, I wonder how many men *really* want children, really know what they want, or ever think about . . ."

"And how many are really good fathers? Dad was an exception."

"Thinking back, well at first he wanted children because I did, but later it was all that religion. He needed a family to share what he'd discovered, or re-created I should say." She glanced in the rearview mirror after the light changed. "Before you were born, before your father began teaching himself Hebrew and whatnot, it was history. I can remember him reading Graetz's *History of the Jews*. And volume after volume of Salo Baron—he bought each new book as soon as it came out. He'd have one of those navy blue volumes with him all the time, in white book jackets that were dirty and torn. Of course, since he'd bring them everywhere—the beach, the dentist, the gas station." Mildred lowered the air-conditioning vent. "Too much direct air. But it all started back during the war, if I'm not wrong. With the first newspaper stories of the Holocaust. He read everything. There were my relatives in Europe to think about, but your father, well, more than anybody else around here—he took it all so, how can I put it? So personally."

"He took everything personally. Remember when we used to study together on *Shabbes*, he'd dissect the text as though it were written just for us, like a garbled telegram addressed to him. Maybe that's why he studied alone—just with Pearl and me. No courses. It was too personal for groups, for classes full of people who didn't think there was anything intimate about the Exodus."

Driving up Middle Turnpike. The synagogue appeared on the right. Trees and shrubs huddled around it, tall and green. Ida always pictured the neglected lots that surrounded the temple when she was growing up. Like a desert with tents. Slanted tin roofs rose to different heights above the Hebrew school, auditorium, and sanctuary.

"When they were building the temple, I used to climb up there and read in the sun. Between the roof and the flat area. I read *The Grapes of Wrath* there. Did you know that?"

"God, Ida. Both you and your father, may he rest in peace, were always sort of peculiar. Only Pearl and I were normal."

Inside the sanctuary Ida gazed at the sand-colored walls and blond wood, and upward at the boxed skylight that turned darker when clouds blocked the sun. At the front of the pulpit stood a tortured modern menorah of hammered brass with branches growing up toward the light like a cactus bearing bulbs of fruit. Royal blue upholstery on the *bima* seats and two new tapestries—a multicolored burning bush and an abstract depiction of the Ten Commandments—interrupted the moderate tan tones. To Ida, this was the house of the book, her father's book. Once the service began, she could sink into the prayer book, submerged. Below her mother's concerns and the greetings of congregants.

Ida lingered on the opening pages. "Who sustains and comforts in times of trouble and distress. Who frees the bound and supports the fallen and raises the bowed." Drifting back to Middle Turnpike, Ida remembered the leafy boughs passing by the window as her mother drove. Passing . . . We're sorry he passed away. Don't look at the squashed squirrel in the road. Try not to.

"And if you listen to the commandments . . ."

"*L'dor v'dor . . .*"

"All of the commandments . . ."

"From generation to generation . . ."

"*Ezrat avotaynu . . .*"

"From generation to generation . . ."

"The help of our fathers . . ."

"From Egypt He redeemed us."

"He who makes peace in the heavens, He will make peace

on earth." To make peace with it—without it, without Rob, without a child. In October she would be thirty-nine. October twelfth.

"Ida dear. Here comes Mrs. Mozer. You remember her, don't you? Gallstones, lately."

"*Mechayei maytim.* Who brings life to the dead." To give life. "From generation to generation." The words of the prayers echoed behind Mildred's whispers. "Don't forget to ask Helen Fine how her husband is feeling."

"Redeem us for a blessing, and save us for life." Ida plodded through the Hebrew from page to page, translating into the blunt, direct English she and her father had wed to the ancient words. "Our eyes shall see a return to Zion." Although it was not the beginning of a month, Ida silently read the psalm recited on the new moon while the rest of the congregation began the Torah service. She did not want to skip anything, miss anything.

". . . He makes the childless woman of the house a happy mother of children." How? When? Here in Your house, *Beit Shalom,* the House of Peace. Where is my peace?

On the pulpit, the holy scroll had been removed from the ark. The rabbi paused with his pointer, searching for the first line of the weekly passage. "Today's Torah portion is taken from the book of Deuteronomy, chapters 29 and 30. We call it *Nitzavim,* which means 'stand,' from the first line of the reading. 'You are *standing* here today, all of you, before the Lord your God.' "

Ida began reading from the Bible in her lap as the rabbi chanted from the Torah. ". . . that you should cross over into the covenant of the Lord your God . . ."

L'avrechah, from the root *avore,* like *Ivrit*—Hebrew. Hebrews—the people who cross over. Cross, contradict, transgress.

"Pearl wrote that the baby's almost sleeping through the night. Imagine that. And doesn't the rabbi look thin, Ida? He's never been the same after that operation."

Ida rushed through the blessings that punctuated the Torah reading, quietly continuing by herself, ahead of the others, translating.

> ...And it will come upon you all these things, the blessing and the curse, which I give you .... And the Lord your God will open your heart and the heart of your seed to love .... And you shall pay attention and hear the voice of the Lord and do all His commandments that I command you today.

How? "Be fruitful and multiply," it says in Genesis, the first commandment. My first desire.

"And the Lord your God will make you abundant ... in the fruit of your body ... because God will return to rejoice over you for good as He rejoiced over your father."

She looked up at the menorah. Her sister had been in labor for twenty hours before Artie was born. When Ida first saw her nephew's face, it was bruised from the forceps. Pearl had named the baby after her father. And the baby had her father's eyes. Whose eyes did Ida have? Who would ever have her eyes?

> For this commandment that I command you today is not too hard for you and not too far off .... Because very close to you is the thing, in your mouth and in your heart, and you may do it .... You shall live and you shall multiply .... Life and death I give before you, the blessing and the curse, and choose life so that you and your seed shall live.

"Choose life."

Ida joined the congregation for the songs that accompanied the return of the Torah scrolls to the ark, but she kept her finger inside the closed blue Bible. During the standing devotion, she opened it again to her marked place. *Habrachah v'haklalah*—the blessing and the curse. She carefully placed the crimson ribbon from the top of the binding down the shiny page.

Finally, the rabbi introduced the special lines said by those who had just lost a loved one or were commemorating the anniversary of a death.

> Almighty and eternal Father, in adversity as in joy—Thou, our source of life, art ever with us. As we recall with affection those whom Thou hast summoned, we thank Thee for the example of their lives, for our sweet companionship with them, for the cherished memories they leave behind. May their souls be bound up with the bond of life. In solemn testimony to that unbroken faith which links the generations one to another, let those who mourn or observe a *yartzeit* now rise to recite the *Kaddish* and sanctify Thy holy name.

Ida stood beside her mother.

2

If only she had brought an umbrella. Ida hailed a cab and dripped into the back seat. "Lowell Street in Northwest, please. Go up Connecticut Avenue past the bridge over Rock Creek Park, then left on Macomb and again on 35th."

"It's going to take a while, Ma'am, with this traffic and the rain. Seems as though everybody is either coming or going today at National. The airport's awful busy for a Monday afternoon."

The taxi crossed Memorial Bridge. Ida remembered the load of clothes she hadn't finished last week before leaving. The laundry basket she wanted to use was cluttered with Rob's clean socks. More than he needed to bother taking. Soft black mounds, identical, stuffed with themselves. In the washroom, on the chair in the hall, under the sofa—like the droppings of a giant stuffed bunny.

Rob would not stop over without calling. They had agreed. But the refrigerator was stocked with his pineapple juice, and his winter clothes were in the upstairs closet. Sheila's apartment was small, he said. They would probably move when her lease expired next fall. So his skis were still in the basement, his poster collection in the bedroom. Ida decided to sleep in the den.

"Yes, that's right. It's the first house with yellow shutters."

The garage. Maybe this would be a good time to clean

it out. Not too large—just big enough for one car. And with the door open, it would almost be like working outside. For hours. But it was so dirty, and the bikes and rakes and the heavy wheelbarrow.

"Right here is fine. What do I owe you?"

The grass had been mowed. Rob must have been over during the weekend. What if he were there now? Maybe he called and found no one home and stopped by for his tennis racket. Or his canceled checks. But his car was not in the driveway.

"Thank you, Ma'am. Any time you need a ride, here's my card—Washington Cab, ask for Willy. You sure I can't help with those bags?"

Ida fumbled for her keys, trying two or three before she found the right one. Inside, some letters were scattered on the floor beneath the mail chute. Not enough for four days. Neat piles of letters on the dining room table showed that Rob had sorted out his.

She gathered the envelopes from the floor. A bill from Woodward and Lothrop peeking through its frosted window, an overdue notice from the library, an orange invitation addressed in flowery script to Mr. and Mrs. Weiss, and a typed envelope with Boston University letterhead. Special delivery.

"This is it." Ida sat down on the stairs.

Dear Dr. Morgan-Weiss:

Our committee was most pleased with your materials and your interview, and in view of the extremely late date, we voted Friday afternoon. I wanted to inform you immediately. On behalf of the department and the university, I wish to offer you a position

Ida stopped reading. "Offer you a position." Four words stood between her and all the cans of pineapple juice. Four words to cancel the free fall through an empty week. There was still time to call U-Haul and reserve a trailer for tomorrow. Spend the evening separating old clothes for Goodwill and packing into boxes what she wanted to keep. What to store in the attic, or in her mother's cedar chest? "To offer you a position." The bill of passage out of Lowell Street. She wanted to recite it, secure it. Under a paperweight of words. "Oh, Rob, I got the job . . ." Come over to the house? Out for a drink, or dinner? And then come home alone, or not . . . until later. No.

The phone rang.

"It's Rose. I just got back from Cleveland. It kills me, I don't leave Boston all summer and then need to be out of town the week of your interview! You haven't heard yet, have you?"

"I got it."

"Oh, Ida. That's wonderful! When are you moving up?"

"Well, I might as well pack up right away and drive up some time tomorrow. I can start looking for a place as soon as I get there. I have to be back in Connecticut for the weekend. Friday night is Rosh Hashanah, you know."

"What a way to start the new year!"

"Can I stay with you until I find a place?"

Rose spoke slowly, with space around her words. Extra room, like her large dress size. But Ida had never thought of her as overweight. "Who's helping you, Ida?"

"Well, I just got the letter. Just now. But the teenage boys next door could give me a hand with any lifting, and if they get a few of their friends, it shouldn't take long."

In the silence over the receiver Ida could hear the radio

announcer in Rose's apartment. The old-fashioned radio—a rectangle with rounded edges—sat on Rose's kitchen counter.

"And I suppose you'll call Rob to come over and divide up things."

"Uh, actually, I think I'll just do it myself. He said I could have whatever I wanted. Maybe I'll call him after I make a list of any things in question." Like the Encyclopedia Britannica or the blender or the long-sleeve flannel workshirt.

"My dear Ida. How about the watercolor you two bought in Paris? You'll keep that, won't you? Remember, we got the frame for it in that little antique shop when I came to visit."

The Parisian boutique where Ida bought Rose the souvenir gray elephant made out of shells. They all had laughed when they got it home and saw the label underneath: MADE IN THE BAHAMAS. The elephant with the eyes of a Buddha.

"Ida, I have another idea. How about meeting me at the Baltimore airport this evening. I can take the last flight. There's some business I've been meaning to handle in New York, anyway, which I could do in a few hours on Wednesday. It would break up the trip. We could share the driving that way. Give yourself another day, Ida. And listen, you know how well we work together wrapping glasses in newspaper. Remember when you helped me pack for the move to Chicago?"

They had also moved out of the dorm together and taken their first apartment, a small duplex in Watertown. Rose and Ida had folded sweaters into the same boxes two years later when Ida left to marry Rob.

"I've been thinking, Ida. I haven't had a roommate in

sixteen years now. And I don't need a study, really. I could move the desk into my bedroom. How about it?"

How about it? The peculiar intonation in Rose's voice, nearly an octave between the high and low notes of her register. How about it, Ida? That crochet looks like a fishnet for whales. Pearl's baby would fall right through it, along with her mother and a couple of neighbors. How about we rip it out and start again? I'll show you. Ida remembered her friend's fleshy, freckled hands.

"Have you got room for my name on your mailbox?"

"Probably not. We can write it on the door. Morgan-Weiss and Grandby—sounds like a law firm."

"Bless you, Rose. I . . ."

"We can talk later. You get to work sorting out your closet. A safe job—all the junk in there is yours. I'll call you back as soon as I book a flight."

3

The straggly trees on Brookline Street were shedding their speckled leaves even though September was hardly two weeks old. Boston had suffered a blistering summer that had finally burned itself out. Ida sat at her window, staring outside at the stunted front porch. The face of her new house, snubbing its nose at the dry foliage. At dawn, the white clapboard shingles appeared pale green. "Rose must still be asleep."

A stack of lined index cards on the night table. Ida reached for them. "What are the humanities?" She always printed neatly on the first few cards, in bold letters. "Cicero, the great orator of the first century before the Common Era, insisted that the humanities are incentives to noble action."

The first day of school. Ida recalled earlier anniversaries of this occasion when her feet had chafed in new saddle shoes below a starched petticoat and plaid jumper; cool mornings with warmer afternoons, dragging a white cardigan and the first, neatly lined sheets of grainy paper with her signature and date in the right-hand corner, along with stories about a new teacher whose name she'd forgotten. Even then Ida had felt that school started as soon as she left the house. Today, her much rehearsed lecture would begin in the car rather than at the lectern.

"The humanities offer clues but never a complete answer. They reveal how people have tried to make sense of a world in which irrationality, despair, loneliness and death are as conspicuous as birth, friendship, hope and reason." Ida squinted to read the lines she'd scrawled on the third card. "Why can't I remember to print!"

"*Guten morgen,* Ms. Morgan. An omelet on toast awaits you."

"Rose, I didn't know you were up. Eggs? Oh, how nice of you to make me breakfast."

"As befits this first day at academe. Stand up and turn around. Hmm. Off-white cotton knit. Pumps with low heels. Very smart, Dr. Weiss. You look nice."

They sat down at the small kitchen table. Rose poured coffee. "I couldn't let you go off without a proper meal. For the last three days you've been gearing up like an athlete in training."

Ida reached for the salt. "One person from each division will be speaking to the whole freshman class on 'the essence of the discipline,' in Mast's words. As the new kid on the block, I've been asked to speak for humanities."

"Why? Because you were the only person not at last year's faculty meeting to vote for someone else?"

Ida cleared the table and began washing the dishes.

"Will you be nervous?"

"Only the first time, and that was days ago. In my imagination I've delivered my talk ten, maybe fifteen times since then—the first five to learn it, five more to forget it. Now I can speak extemporaneously with the illusion of déjà vu."

"Ah, the gymnastics of the mind! So you'll enjoy giving it?"

"Well, afterwards, anyway. For now I can't get it to stop playing over and over again in my head." Ida wrapped the dishcloth around her hand and held it up like a microphone. "Through the humanities we learn how individuals and societies define the moral life. Through the humanities we learn how individuals and societies define the moral life. Through the humanities . . ."

Rose put the plastic placemats back on the clean table. "We seem to be experiencing some technical difficulties. And now for a word from our sponsor."

Ida walked into Rose's room to check the full-length mirror on the back of the door. "You know, Rose, when I look in the mirror these days, I keep expecting to see you; I'm startled for a second when I recognize myself instead. It used to happen to me years ago, too, when we lived in the dorm. Remember? Rose, do you ever think that we look alike?" Ida turned to see if she'd hemmed her skirt evenly in the back.

"Just alike, give or take fifty pounds!" Rose reached for a jar of hand cream she kept near the sink.

"Come on, Rose. You know I didn't mean that. But they say that people who live together start to resemble each other."

"In other words, have I noticed that my hair is getting curlier, or darker? Or maybe you're growing taller—what, six inches or so? I think that broken humanities record you've been playing has dulled your needle. Are you feeling okay, Ida?" Rose joined Ida in the bedroom. "I've always thought we were exceedingly dissimilar, to tell you the truth. Holy Mary and Joseph! Here we have a sophisticated city girl and a country hick." Rose avoided the mirror.

"Connecticut isn't the sticks, Rose."

"Un huh. A lapsed Irish Catholic and a closet Jew."

"I'd hardly call my Judaism closeted."

"A physical therapist and a doctor of the mind."

"Rose, be serious." Ida stepped away from the door. "Do you have a necklace or something I could wear with this top? Outside the collar?"

"Sure, try my coral strand." Ida looked in the upper part of Rose's jewelry box. "And then, of course, there's our similar family background—my father was a drunk, and yours was in danger of being canonized."

"Jews don't do that, Rose."

"And we all know what Catholics don't do."

Ida checked her watch. "I better get going." Brightening, "When I get home tonight, this will be all over! Now don't you forget, Rose—through the humanities we learn how societies . . ."

"Oh, get out of here already, will ya?" Rose turned the coral around Ida's neck so that the clasp was in the back.

Since Brookline was a one-way street, Ida headed a short block toward Central Square and turned right on Pacific. Not a single structure on either side of the road. She checked the gas gauge: a full tank.

"Through the humanities we learn how individuals and societies define the moral life and . . ." And what? With one hand on the wheel, she felt for the Rockefeller Report she had tried to memorize. Her fingers found the paperclip marking the page. "Damn!" The passage was underlined in red; "and try to attain it, attempt to reconcile freedom and the responsibilities of citizenship, and express them artistically." Ida glanced back up at the road. "And try to attain it. And try to attain it." She followed the alley that separated the blank walls of an industrial complex, coming out at last near the circle at the foot of the B.U. Bridge. "Reconcile. Reconcile." She put down the book on the dashboard next to her note cards. "If I just get that word, the rest will come. Reconcile. Reconcile freedom and the responsibilities of citizenship. F and R. F and R. Freedom and responsibility. Reconcile."

Ida noticed that her clutch no longer stuck when she shifted into second. "Good. It fixed itself. No need to waste any time on this nonsense." She eased the car into the faster-moving traffic and up the ramp. A robin's egg sky shimmered navy in the river.

"What are the humanities?" Ida leaned against the podium as her voice reverberated in the microphone, distant yet familiar to her, like a passport photograph. She listened, as if to a close friend. "Someone? The humanities."

In the third row a curly-haired young man who had been whispering throughout the preceding science introduction was rolling a pencil back and forth across his jeans. He glanced up for a moment and banked his answer off the side wall. "The creations of humanity."

Ida nodded. "But since dogs don't produce very much that's worth examining, this definition doesn't eliminate a whole lot."

A ripple of laughter.

"How about the creations that *establish* our humanity? Perhaps we are human *because* we develop literature and art to mirror our existence. Or transform it." Ida thought of Rob as she turned to her second index card. "Give examples," he always said. "Kids like examples. *I* like examples." Rob was missing her lecture.

"The arts are humanity's signature, the way we sign our name, *human being*, pronounced in symphonic splendor, with conceptual profundity, in radiant color." The student in the third row scribbled across the top corner of his loose-leaf binder and turned it sideways for his neighbor to read. "I have a double and my roommate never showed. You wanta change dorms?"

"The term 'humanism' was coined by Italian scholars of the Renaissance." Ida pictured Rose in the audience. So she could speak to someone she knew. At the back of the auditorium Arnold Mast nodded rhythmically. He's probably thinking I'm being too general. Or that Harrington will think so.

"Today the phrase secular humanism is used with derision by some religious fundamentalists. Would the medieval concentration on human sinfulness be a better tribute to life's omnipotent source?"

The student sitting right below the podium was adjusting her sleeve. A white gauze blouse over a Coppertone commercial. And that penny-colored hair. Like Wendy Ross, one of the popular girls whom Ida had always been afraid to approach. In the seventh grade. What can you say to her at a beach party or right before volleyball?

"Through literature and art we can imagine what it would be like to be someone else living in another time or place, and so we stretch our imaginations and enrich our experience. Thus we increase our human potential." One student at the center of the hall was taking notes furiously, and William Harrington smiled. Ida stared at a boy slouching in the end seat to her left. In bibbed overalls and a hat. "You, in the black hat, what do you think? Is this course going to make you more human?" He touched the brim in mock salute. A hat to be underneath. To be seen in. To be seen.

"The humanities as humanizers. In an increasingly dehumanized world, they can be life-support systems. Life-preservers." To hell with Harrington! Skip the Cicero. "The humanities can save your life." An earnest face in the front row. "Do you believe that? What's your name?"

"Marshall Flask."

"Marshall, do you think the humanities ever saved

anyone?" Ida responded herself, mimicking a lower voice, "What is she trying to feed us, anyway?" A chuckle from the rear.

Stepping away from the lectern, "I'll tell you, I was once arrested while traveling in East Germany, and Herman Melville came to my assistance." Not a sound in the auditorium. "You know how? I suddenly thought of Bartleby the Scrivener, a character who totally confounded the bureaucratic mentality. Melville's story helped me gain release." Harrington scowled. But why should they listen to someone they don't even know? A little self-revelation, a promise of intimacy. The admission of vulnerability. "We'll be reading 'Bartleby the Scrivener' this year."

Ida returned to her notes on the wooden stand to which she was tied by the umbilical cord of the microphone. "So am I telling you that you should study humanities for future guidance in escapes from repressive regimes?" She looked down at her outline for the last time. "Probably not. I am saying that you will store your reading for future reference. A person from a novel may someday illuminate a relationship you're having, a landscape from a painting may return to you one summer evening and heighten your enjoyment of a similar view, or you may share a poem with a friend after it offered you solace in a time of loss. Most of all, after glimpsing others through the lens of literature or art, you may turn the glass around and see yourself more clearly. In that sense the humanities can help you survive."

She reached for the Rockefeller Report and her memorized lines. Something solid to hold on to. Below her, shifting in his seat, the boy in the black hat stretched.

"Nice lecture." He walked into her office. "Picasso, right?" motioning at the poster Ida had hung opposite the window. "I like analytic Cubism."

"I'm not sure *I* do, but it's the only thing they had at the Harvard Coop that wasn't too expensive and would match these walls." Phil Manning—she remembered his name.

Phil ran his fingers over the fresh identification plaque on the door. "Morgan-Weiss, is the hyphen for a maiden name?"

"You mean, am I married." The new words tasted like old pennies. Ida held them in her mouth for a moment, rolling them around. Loose change. "Not any more."

"I'm sorry." He scuffed the floor as though a piece of gum were stuck there.

"*Are* you?"

"I have an idea. Let's celebrate the end of the first day of school on the Concord River. I know a place that rents canoes. Want to come?"

"That sounds wonderful." But she wished he had said tomorrow. She'd paced herself to relax by four o'clock. Sip tea with Rose, recap her presentation, rehearse the next day's classes. React, recede, recant, redress. Regret. "I'm not really dressed for it." Retreat, respite, refute.

"So we'll cancel the photographer."

Reread, regress. "Couldn't we put it off till Thursday and I'll bring slacks?" Relinquish, reward, reconcile.

"I'm not free Thursday."

Reluctantly, Ida let a precious piece of after turn into

another dreaded before. Postmortems postponed. "Sure, just give me a few seconds to gather up some books and close out things here. I'll meet you back in your office." Rewrite, rethink, research. The old word game from Girl Scouts. Three minutes—the longest *re* list wins. Go.

Ida reprimanded herself as she looked through the bookcase for the drama anthology to take home in her briefcase. Cowardice, this secondhand fixation! Or art? Recorded in print or paint, the hallowed haunt of second times.

"Hallowed haunt." She took her new grade book out of the middle drawer. "Too pedantic, like 'symphonic splendor and conceptual profundity.' " Her lecture echoed faintly as she locked up the desk.

The South Bridge Boathouse slipped backward as the canoe headed downstream. Up ahead a white home perched on green slopes that eased into the river with a sprinkling of ducks. A balanced composition for paint-by-numbers. Ida's left hand curved over the top of the paddle as she pulled with her right against the water. Thick and opaque with smooth waves, like pudding just before it boils. The water parted at the bow, sliding along the sides of the boat. Barely a ripple where it split for the front of the canoe and rejoined at the rear.

The river curved sharply and then ran straight. Putting-green lawns became shrubs and underbrush. Trees leaned inward from the banks. On the right at a distance—the Concord Academy. A boy's shout was muffled by bird calls and rustling branches.

"Let me do the work for a while." Phil cut a wide J-stroke. Ida stopped paddling and leaned back. She trailed her hand over the side in the cool water.

"I usually come here alone. Out here—nothing else exists. *This* is real—the way the water smells, that hissing sound from the grasses. It pulls me out of . . . Intellectuals spend too much time in their minds. It's stuffy there." Phil moved off the low seat and onto his knees.

"That's why I like airplanes."

"Airplanes? They're even more cramped than offices!" He began to paddle on the other side of the canoe.

"Well, the seats may be. And the windows are small, but the view isn't. From an airplane, nothing too small can be seen."

An arched bridge spanned the river, completing itself in reflection. The curved masonry above and mirrored arc below formed a circle. As the canoe approached the ellipse of stone wedded to its watery memory, the illusion suddenly reversed itself. The lower image seemed solid while its lighter twin became the echo. The boat passed through the center on a film of water.

"Did you see that?" turning back to look at Phil.

"Yes."

Ida settled lower into the hull. Her wrist under the water ached from the cold. She clenched her fist until the knotted fingers grew numb. A piece of hemp was tied to the front of the canoe, and Ida reached for it with her other hand. Pulling back against it. Like the rope tow at Mount Tom. "Hold on, Ida. Just hold on." Rob's terse instructions. Her frozen feet bound in black ski boots, moving forward as long as she squeezed the rope. "Don't let go," her feet slipping on the ice.

Phil lay the paddle across the canoe and leaned forward against it like a bar. Like the handlebars of a bike. "But you can't see any people from the air, or any birds or . . ."

"Yes you can—the people in the plane. And yourself—bigger than ever, larger than the buildings and rivers in the window. You can't run away from yourself in an airplane—you bring yourself along."

The canoe drifted sideways as it floated downstream. "I guess I'm not worried about losing myself in the office or in books." Phil ran his fingers back and forth across the wood. "I'm concerned about losing the world—this world. Not its shadows in thought, but real feeling. After spending the whole day with a little pen, a paddle—well, it fills your whole hand."

At the confluence of a second river, they headed upstream. Calm waters, stagnant on the surface, freckled with leaves and downy seed-puffs. Phil steered the canoe to the middle and stowed the paddle. "Come here, sit with me."

Ida gingerly edged toward the back of the canoe, holding the rim on either side. Then she rested her back against him. The river rocked them together.

They drove through Concord Center and then turned onto Route 2. Ida wrung out the hem of her skirt. Phil glanced in the rearview mirror and then fixed his eyes ahead. On the dashboard a plastic rain bonnet lay folded in a long, thin strip.

"Phil, are you married?" It hadn't occurred to her before. He had no ring, no pictures in his office, no vague "we's" in his syntax.

"Yes, very happily so."

She removed her hands from the seat and stared at the pattern that the cushion had left in her palms. Very happily, Rob must have said, in bed with his darling lawyer. "Then why didn't you bring *her* here instead of me?"

"My wife lives in California. She's an economist and has a major contract out there. We're together over the summer and travel back and forth on vacations."

Ida looked at his face, at the lines that loudly pronounced his age. Late forties, if not fifty.

"Don't you miss her?"

"Of course, but we have wonderful reunions." A playful smirk. "You see, people can't really get together unless they've been apart. That's what's wrong with most marriages, if you ask me." Phil pushed the turn signal a couple of times, trying to get it to work. "Although we aren't roommates right now, Marge is still my best friend." He finally stuck his arm out the window for the right turn. "But that bond isn't dependent on the exclusion of others; real love has its own strength."

"The others, then, are just friends."

"Sometimes." He turned off Storrow Drive at Kenmore Square. The headlights of the oncoming cars glared like flashbulbs.

"She knows that, too? About the friends?"

"Oh, yes."

When they approached the faculty parking lot, Ida began to gather her belongings. "And children?" She released her safety belt.

Phil straightened his arms back from the wheel. "No, she never wanted any."

4

Rose stared at the end table to her left; she tried to choose some suitable reading material. *Parents EXPECTING*, the "parents" in small red letters, "expecting" in yellow capitals. Below the magazine title a slim woman, wearing a red bathing suit and pretending to be pregnant, bounded through the waves beside her mate in ocher trunks. *SEXUALLY TRANSMITTED DISEASES*, a red and orange phosphorescent pamphlet. Next to that, *Your Child Needs—THE BIBLE STORY*, send for free information, no obligation. Rose picked up a plastic-covered copy of *A Doctor Discusses: Making the Mid Years the Prime of Life* (please do not remove from the office). She flipped through the headings: "Sensible Dieting," "Exercise," "A Youthful Attitude." Opposite her in the waiting room a real pregnant woman tried to control two cranky children arguing over a toy car. Rose turned to the bulletin board covered with photographs of infants—eyes tightly closed, drooling or smiling, in white lace bonnets or receiving blankets, held by a grinning Dr. Richmond. Each picture was dated and identified with the baby's last name penned in gold. Blackman, 1970. Christopher, 1968. Shapiro, 1972.

"Mrs. Grandby, the doctor will see you now."

"It's Ms."

"Yes, well just walk down the hall. The conference room is on the far left."

But the doctor was not in the conference room. Another table with more reading matter. Mostly books this time. *American Folklore and Legend, Normal Fetal Development, The Ocean World of Jacques Cousteau, Discover* magazine—the lead story, "Breast Cancer: Too Many Radical Mastectomies?" Rose lifted *The Color Atlas of Life Before Birth*. She turned the pages. Glowing against black backgrounds were large, bent heads on bean sprout bodies with hands almost folded, as if in prayer. Huddled cross-legged like Buddhist monks.

The walls in the conference room were papered with framed documents. "*Salutem in Domino*" . . . "certified by the Department of Health and Mental Hygiene" . . . "faithfully served as intern at the Providence Hospital."

Rose tried to picture the man whose pedigree graced the walls. White hair to match his coat, a deep voice. Wings maybe. Forgive me, Father, for I have sinned. Grant me this dispensation. What sin? No need for confession. In the outer office Rose had filled out forms. Intimate details, her body's secrets. Length of monthly period? Intensity of menstrual cramps? Number of tampons used daily during the heaviest flow? Clear or cloudy discharge?

"Well, Ms. Grandby, this is certainly an unusual request." Without a white coat.

"How do you do, Doctor."

He looked at her chart. "You know, this is the first request of this type I've had from a single woman."

"I could have told you I was married, you know, or given my age as thirty-four instead of thirty-nine."

"Yes, you could have."

Rose started the interview over again. "Tell me about artificial insemination."

"What's to tell? You inject sperm into the vagina." Richmond shifted in his chair, crossing one leg over the other. His pant leg pulled well above the top of his shoe. A thin sock stretched tight above a bony ankle.

"To begin with, you could explain the relative effectiveness of the procedure, its cost and risks, the method of finding donors, health qualifications for the recipient, insurance coverage, success ratios, or any other information that strikes you as pertinent." Rose breathed quickly. Small gulps of air to keep her chest from rising.

As he answered, she began to calculate. Fifty dollars for this half hour, then thirty-five for the appointment at the infertility clinic, seventy-five for each insemination session—"three in a row are recommended"—and approximately two hundred for the semen itself. More than five hundred dollars each month that she'd try!

"You see, if you want fresh, it costs seventy-five dollars a straw, and you'd need three straws a shot for each of three consecutive days. The delivery charge for the sperm is fifty to sixty dollars. But if you choose frozen, the price drops to thirty dollars, plus fifteen dollars handling charge and nineteen ninety-five for delivery."

"You'd think it was a rare commodity." Rose thought of the caterer the hospital had hired for last year's Christmas party on the children's ward. The nurses had saved money by ordering the gas balloons and ice cream separately from local distributors.

"Miss Grandby, may I ask you, why do you want to let yourself in for so many problems? A single parent, and at your age? Children are for younger people. They cost a bundle, and they're a heck of a lot of trouble."

Near the doctor's head a mobile of sailboat parts

dangled in front of the framed documents. The only image in a sea of words. "Do you have any children, Dr. Richmond?"

"Yes, four."

"Was it worth it?"

He removed his watch, twisting the expandable strap. "Well, who knows—if I had it to do over again, actually . . ." He stood up and walked to the wastebasket, which he moved closer to the wall. "Probably not, but hindsight, unlike foresight . . ."

"Doctor, I'm a physical therapist. I specialize in children's disabilities, so I work with youngsters every day of my life. I love children. I'm not deciding *whether* to have a baby; I'm trying to decide *how*."

Ida was still thinking of the water against her paddle as she searched for the right key to the front door. First she tried all the bronze ones, but there was no demarcating line on the ring, and after three or four keys she lost track of which direction she was going on the steel circle crowded with metal formulas. Ida was slow to discard old keys, so they jangled heavily together and obscured her choice. At last the lock turned.

"Hi, I'm home."

"Where were you, Ida? Are they working you till dark already the first day?"

"No, one of my colleagues invited me to go canoeing after my lecture."

"Hm, they're starting that soon, are they?" Rose opened the oven to check the casserole she'd prepared.

"Rose, they're not plural. His name's Phil Manning."

Ida began to flip through the mail on the counter. She hadn't yet received many letters at her new address. A pale yellow envelope, smaller than normal size, fell from among Rose's bills. "I saw one from your ex-in-laws." Rose was cutting carrots into the salad.

"I don't think of *them* as ex." Ida turned the letter around several times without opening it. She finally unfolded the thin sheets of translucent paper that were penned in a regular, childlike script on only one side of each sheet.

Dearest Ida,

We spoke to your mother on the phone yesterday, and she told us about your new job. Congratulations and best wishes! Still, Dad was really quite concerned about your moving. We wish you had at least told us about it first. Dad figures that Rob will come to his senses before long, and it would be much easier for him to go back to you if you were still living in the house as though nothing had happened.

(cont. on page 2)

"So what do the senior Weisses have to say?" Rose opened a new box of napkins.

"They think I should pretend that nothing's happened."

"That figures."

Oh, well, I guess you know best. I can't tell you how upset we've been these last few months! We refuse to have anything to do with our son. We can't understand how he could do such a thing—and with a *shiksa*, no less! We just want you to know that we love you and think of you every day.

(cont. on page 3)

"Pretending is very parental." Rose put the forks on top of the folded napkins. "My father used to pretend he had a job while my mother pretended he wasn't pretending. In the meantime, we kids couldn't quite hack it in Never-never Land, and I was much too big to be taken for Tinkerbell."

"Gee, you're in a great mood today. You having trouble at the hospital with the parents of some of your kids? How's that girl doing who was in the car crash?" Ida turned to page 3 of the letter.

The holidays were very hard on us this year. Thinking ahead to Thanksgiving, we wanted to invite you down. Why don't you and your friend Rose come down here together? We'd love to see her, too, and you could have a nice little vacation in the sun. It would mean so much to Doris and the children to have their auntie, at least. Talk it over with Rose. Please call us, dear,—collect, and let us know.

If there's anything we can do for you, at any time, don't hesitate to ask. May God bless!

Much love,
Mom and Dad

P.S. Don't forget to call.

Rose read over Ida's shoulder. "Hey, Auntie Idie dearest. P.S. Serve with plenty of syrup."

"Rose, you're too critical."

"Probably, but you're not critical enough. After all, you too moved in with a *shiksa*!"

Ida heard Bea's voice as she reread the letter. She could see her suntanned skin pulled tight over her flat face. Her eyes small and hazel like Rob's, her voice, like Rob's, a bit too high.

"I suppose I have to go see them. What do you think?"

"I don't know why you feel any obligation. Apparently Rob doesn't."

"On the contrary. I'm just in a better position to fulfill it. I think, on one level, that if Rob had felt less obligation, he might have . . . Wait, I'll make a dressing. You don't have to use the bottled stuff."

Rose and Ida sat down at the table. "It might be nice, though. We could swim a little, perhaps rent a car and drive to the Keys for the weekend . . ." Rose poured some wine.

"That *would* be nice, and I'd feel better about visiting them if you were there as a buffer. You sure you're game? They mean well, but talking to them is like shouting across a canyon. It was pretty bad even before Morris started to lose his hearing."

Rose smiled. "Critical Rose doesn't have to shout. Barking dogs, and all that. You know—the hounds that bellow don't bite, but the ones that are really potent . . .

Anyway, since they're not my relatives, I haven't much need to hear them. For me it would be time spent with you."

"So, Rose, tell me about your day." And then she saw it, like a boulder in the road. Ida had been thoughtfully walking, staring down at her own feet. Not looking up. "Rose, what?"

She finished clearing the table. "Let's wait till we're done with the dishes. We can talk in the living room."

Ida curled her feet under her on the sofa. Rose sat opposite the couch in an upholstered chair.

"I went to the doctor today."

"Rose, are you all right?"

"I'm fine. I saw an obstetrician."

An obstetrician. The word echoed in Ida's ears as in the chambers of a seashell. An obstetrician. Bouncing off the calcareous surface, turning in the tapering spiral. "Are you . . . but who?"

"Oh, Ida. There's no one else. Just me and my need for a child."

And the child that Rob had never wanted: "Because I have no desire to turn into my father. Because I don't need to tell someone else what to do. Because I can't even stand my sister's kids."

Rose reached for a magazine left on the coffee table and returned it to the wooden newspaper rack. "I haven't talked to you about it lately because—what with your losing Rob and all, I thought . . . But these last few months, it's been coming to a head for me. I made a decision—actually, I spent the whole past year coming to the realization that I had a decision to make." Ida's hands loosened in her lap, and she gazed at the empty space cradled between her fingers. "And maybe, too, I stopped sharing it with you because I had to reach this point alone, to feel the full weight of the issue and my ability to handle it."

"How, Rose? Who will father it?"

"Of course, that's the first problem. If I had a man that I loved, or even a close male friend . . . Originally I thought of Morton Ashley back in Chicago, you remember him. But even if I felt *I* could do that, he's been living with Michael for ten years now." Smoothing her skirt like pants around her legs, "It might be unfair even to ask. I wouldn't want to offend Morton or put him in an uncomfortable position—to tell the truth, I don't know if he's *ever* been with a woman."

Ida tried to picture Morton and Rose in any position. Morton Ashley, with his black eyes and beautiful poems and thin arms like a praying mantis. With as much body as a thought.

"Two novices, we'd probably screw it up!" Rose turned the large ring of a silver bracelet around on her wrist. "I've been thinking of my own mother. One baby right after another, before she was twenty-five. She couldn't stop; my problem is in starting."

"And the obstetrician? You went already?" Digging into the mound of pillows, Ida made a hollow for her back in the corner of the couch.

"Now, Ida, didn't your mother tell you that babies come from doctors? *Doctor* is the answer when the kid asks: 'What's a stork?' " Rose took the crocheted afghan from the arm of the chair and opened it in her lap. "Nowadays, you're supposed to see a doctor before, during, and after."

"Come on, Rose."

"Well, if it comes to that, I can always find just—someone. But I'd rather take the medical route, in a doctor's office." With Dr. Richmond presiding. Rose could still see his clerical smile and thin hair. "The modern world has really come of age, hasn't it? We can now order immaculate conception—in my case, complete with virgin birth!" Her airy laugh was like the rustle of tissue paper around a present.

"Oh Rose, I'm so happy for you! Well, what shall we do? Buy champagne? Go to a bookstore and find some paperbacks on infant care?" Ida looked at the space under the window across from the fireplace. Where a playpen could go. "Rose . . . we're really going to have a baby? A real baby? Here? In our house!" A crib and a high chair and a padded changing table, like Pearl's. "A real baby!"

"My decision isn't all there is to it, Ida. Unfortunately. I have to convince my doctor, or find another to lie to, and then there's the politics of dealing with the infertility clinic, and then, needless to say, we have to pray that it works, and keep trying and paying for who knows how long."

"When do you start?"

"*I've* started. Tomorrow I begin recording my morning temperature to chart the time of ovulation. As soon as it goes up, we're on." Rose leaned back in the chair she filled, her heavy arms and legs spilling over the bulky lounger. "Ida, I feel, well, quiet. Like when a noise you haven't really noticed finally stops."

Twenty students sat around the conference table, notebooks open, books closed, a breeze blowing in from the window. Ida had been a little late. She sat down at the far end.

"We've finished our introductory unit on imagery and symbolic language. Today we begin our first major topic of the year—the tragic, comic, and ironic visions as contrasting literary modes. Sophocles' *Oedipus Rex*, which you've all read for today, will serve as our initial study in tragedy."

A few of the students did not fit around the long table and sat separately against the back wall. Closest to the door, a boy cupped his hand just below his nose and spoke loudly to his neighbor.

"What, Adam?" Ida pushed aside her note pad.

"Can I be honest with you, Professor? I was just saying to Jason here, this stuff is as bad as . . . I mean, what are we supposed to get out of this? Here's a guy who accidentally kills his father and sleeps with his mother, just like some fortune-teller predicted he would, and so they kick him out as king and he gouges out his eyes."

"The official *Readers' Digest* version. Geared to the slow reader." Pat Hollusk had a dry voice. He always sat to Ida's right. Hollusk, she had tried to remember. Like mollusk. A little shell, hard and pat.

"Okay, Patrick, Adam's synopsis is short on subtlety, but he's got the bare bones. Let's start with the skeleton."

Pat put one hand on his biceps while rotating his arm as though he had a cramp. "Ribs, anyone? A backbone?"

"A backbone—the fortune-teller, the concept of fate, if you will." Ida walked to the board and wrote the word *oracle*. "The playwright postulates that men are doomed to murder their fathers and pursue their mothers. What's that, a peculiarity of ancient Athens?"

"Oh, so *that's* where the term Oedipus complex came from."

"Right, Susan. Twenty-five centuries later Freud made this concept the cornerstone of modern psychology. Let's look beneath the surface of this story." Ida put the chalk down in the double tray and rubbed the white powder off her index finger. Where a sliver had been. From the canoe. She could feel the wooden rim, and Phil's legs on either side of her. With flat knees.

"I found the play annoying because there was nothing Oedipus could do to change his fate. He was trapped. When his parents were told what the gods anticipated, they got rid of their son, and then Oedipus was raised by another couple *he* thought were his real parents. Like, it was all rigged ahead of time. That made me mad." He tried to fit the stub of an eraser back into the end of his pencil.

"Ed, turn to page 64, for a moment. Everyone, open your books. If Oedipus weren't really to blame for his predicament, why does he say at the end—look, find the line: 'This curse was laid on me by no one but myself'? He assumes responsibility for his actions. What did he do wrong?" She gave them time to find the passage. "Now, in a famous philosophical treatise, Aristotle wrote that the tragic hero has a fatal flaw that brings about the person's downfall. What was this man's character defect?" Thunder, with cymbals played by brushes—outside the window, the subway line ran above ground. The floor in the classroom vibrated. "Come on, somebody give it a try."

Carol stopped writing. The frizzed ends of her permanent quivered when she spoke. "I think he should have left well enough alone. If he hadn't asked so many questions, if he hadn't taken things into his own hands—you know, if he'd stayed at home and not tried to get to the bottom of everything, like digging into the past, nothing would have happened to him."

Ed sat one seat away from Carol. "Yeah, you said it—nothing. He never would have become king, either."

Ida walked by her own chair and around the table. She stopped behind Carol. "Perhaps leaders or heroes are those people who persist in trying to solve the riddles that others avoid. Any more ideas about where Oedipus went wrong?" She looked at Adam.

"The man was a real hothead. I mean, somebody pushes him in the road, and right away he kills the guy. He overreacts all the time."

Mark raised his hand. "But don't you think he was a good king, overall? I felt sorry for him. He didn't deserve it."

Pat: "Well, that's the whole point. Otherwise it wouldn't be tragic. One flaw spoils all his exceptional qualities and does him in."

"Dr. Morgan, what's the bit about the riddle, the one he first answers to become king? In high school we learned the question—What goes on four legs in the morning, two in the afternoon, and three in the evening? Oedipus guessed that the answer is 'man' since a baby crawls, a mature person walks upright, and in old age you use a cane; what's that *really* all about, symbolically?"

Ida answered Howard's question with more questions. "What was the nature of the query? What is the substance of the answer? Carol?"

"That people change."

"Yes. Good. Notice, too, that the first question Oedipus addresses is 'What is man?' The next one he faces is 'Who am I?' He needs to know where he came from. What type of question is this?" Ida picked up Carol's book from the table.

Raymond: "History?"

Carol: "Identity."

"Precisely. Oedipus is compelled to solve the mystery of his birth, the secret of his origins." Ida looked at her watch. They were running out of time. She wondered if Phil would be back in his office. "Let me leave you with one observation. Otto Rank wrote a book in which he claims that many leaders, as depicted in a host of cultural traditions, are strikingly similar with respect to birth and childhood. One way or another, the parents who raise them are not the parents responsible for their births. Oedipus is the son of Jocasta and Laius, but he is adopted by Polybus and Merope. Likewise, Moses was the child of Israelite slaves who was brought up in the Egyptian pharaoh's palace. Romulus and Remus, the legendary founders of ancient Rome, were supposedly suckled by wolves, and even Jesus was not *really* Joseph's son insofar as Christian theology maintains that Mary was a virgin impregnated directly by the Holy Spirit. So, why? Why are all these critical figures adoptees?"

Peter was already on his feet, turning the sleeve of his jacket inside out. "Perhaps they feel less secure and strive harder to compensate."

"Perhaps."

"Or they're doubly endowed, from two sources rather than only one."

"Well, it highlights the whole problem of heredity versus environment. Maybe they combine the best of both."

"Sometimes they're treated badly, which builds character."

"Or treated better, as special, different. They have to be different from the followers in order to lead them."

The door opened and closed as the next class checked again to see if Ida's students had begun leaving.

Ida walked toward the window. "Perhaps these twice-born people, so to speak, acquire a certain double vision. They are heirs to two heritages and are ever conscious that things might have turned out otherwise." Outside, the MTA stopped at the intersection. Like a fat, green caterpillar slow to start, with people trickling out of its mouth. "Possibly, double origins are an antidote to simplistic, automatic thinking. A second situation interjects the notion of the conditional. 'What if I'd remained with my first set of parents?' 'What if I'd had another upbringing?' 'What if I'd . . .' "

Ida dismissed the class.

Standing by her car and shivering, she felt through the compartments of her pocketbook for the keys. "This is positively the last day for short sleeves. Tomorrow is wool."

"Indian summer is waving good-bye. It won't be long now." Phil Manning's car was parked next to Ida's. "Since I've successfully found my keys, why don't you join me in *my* car?"

Ida kept searching. Perhaps they'd fallen into the section she reserved for pencils. "And go where?"

"To one of my favorite places in the fall. Minute Man National Park. We can walk up to the old mansion there and watch the sun set."

Ida stopped hunting and looked up. "After which we'll be in the dark, right?"

He was leaning against the hood. "But then you'll have a good reason why you can't find your keys." The back wall of the school was reflected in his windshield, curving so that the whole building fit between the wipers and the roof. "So, what do you say?"

"Well, okay. Actually, it sounds very nice."

His car smelled like the inside of an old wallet. Well worn leather, rubbed smooth. Like the close shave on his familiar face. Mildred Morgan used to tell babysitters that her daughter didn't like strangers. "Stop by the house a few times—just sit in a chair and let her look at you. The third time you come she'll think you're one of the family."

The ride was short.

"Have you ever been to the Old Manse?" He closed the door on the driver's side without bothering to lock it.

"*Mosses From an Old Manse*. God, this is where Nathaniel Hawthorne wrote. Right over there!"

Phil put his arm over Ida's shoulder as they kicked two paths through the leaves. Giant tree trunks rose like columns to hold up the sky.

"This is my idea of a Gothic cathedral." Phil ran his hand across the rough bark.

"I can understand that. Those churches are like forests; they both make you feel dwarfed. At first. And then free and soaring when you look up."

A winding path beside the house led down to a bridge over low water.

"That's where they fired the shot heard round the world, the British on this side, the colonists on the other." Phil pointed to an obelisk—an index finger of granite marking the exact location. Ida read from its pedestal. "Here, on the nineteenth day of April 1775, was made the first forcible resistance to British aggression. Upon the opposite bank stood the American militia. Here stood the invading army, and on this spot the first of the enemy fell in the war of revolution that gave independence to these United States." She slid her knuckles along the polished stone. "Here. Right here. Only with smaller trees. And the house?"

"Yes, that too. The home was owned by Emerson's grandfather before Hawthorne rented it." Phil put both hands in his back pockets.

"Emerson, Hawthorne—on this same dirt. I read what they wrote and hold the same thoughts in my mind. The exact words. Yet where are those men now?"

He started to walk. "Landmarks and literature—they're markers at the edges. Beware, abyss on either side!" With heel to toe, he mimed a tightrope walker. The imitation went on too long. Finally, pretending to lose his balance, he grabbed for Ida to steady himself.

Up ahead a piece of slate, framed by chained pillars, memorialized the grave of two British soldiers.

They came three thousand miles and died
To keep the past upon its throne,
Unheard beyond the ocean tide
Their English mother made her moan.

Ida charged through the singsong verse with an epitaph of *owns*. Blown and drone and groan alone. "Not just earth and art, but the seeds of ourselves. The parents of your parents' parents, their great-grandparents, were here—or somewhere else—reading about this, perhaps, at least sharing the calendar date. A chain of flesh back to the beginning. Never broken, until now. Soon, anyway. Does that bother you, too?" She stooped to pick the wispy white afterthought of a dandelion growing at the base of the concrete posts. "Like me, you too are a last link."

"I know."

"Do you think about it often?"

"No." He tucked his shirt into the back of his pants. "The past and present are enough to keep me busy. The future is fiction."

Ida saw a side loop that his belt had missed and hooked her finger through it. "A useful attitude when you have to plan ahead."

"I don't."

They crossed the wooden bridge.

"Daniel Chester French." Ida recognized the statue of the Minute Man from the frontispiece of an old social studies text.

"Correct for two points. Your next question . . ."

"Gee, I used to look at that page a lot. Whenever I wasn't listening. Grammar school with Mrs. Carra."

"You were a model student, I see." Phil looked behind him across the bridge. "You know, whenever I come here I notice this—an abstract shape, that little pyramid over there, marks the British casualties while the Minute Man represents our dead. One's own loss is human, with a face. Another's pain is conceptual."

They started up an incline toward a second house, a brick mansion of later vintage.

"Wait, Ida. Look." The abutting hillside was red and orange. Only a tinge of green in the brilliant, dying leaves. Scarlet in the sunset. Ida leaned closer to Phil. He turned and kissed her.

Lips, soft and large, overlapping her own. Rob's lips were thinner, Ida's on the outside, his tongue pointed. Fifteen years of a pointed tongue. Ida put her hands on Phil's chest to hold him back. She shut her eyes when he traced his fingers around the edge of her mouth. Against her face she could feel his hand, but her lips were numb. Thin, translucent, like scar tissue. Ida had cut Rob out of her life with the blunt scissors from the second grade, leaving a wide margin all around him.

Phil's hand on the back of her head and neck, under her hair, and his lips again, barely moving on hers. So still, it was not a kiss but a mouth. Phil's mouth. Phil. No advance, no retreat. Behind her closed eyelids, Ida stared into the orange darkness toward Phil, close to her, just on the other side. His wide tongue covered hers.

Near the top of the hill they climbed over a fence and sat in the meadow. Growing darker. The outlines of shrubs and trees were smudged. Brown dust, like sediment stirred up from the bottom of a river, seemed to rise from the ground. Ida told Phil about Rose and the baby. "She brings it all back for me, all that time when my husband's objections and my desire for a child crowded out everything else. Like a cancer in remission—and now it's back. I feel cheated, robbed."

"Worse than that—it sounds to me, because now you're an accomplice in theft. Since Rose's child won't have to be a gift from someone else. Maybe you robbed yourself?"

Ida looked at the blunt end of his fingernails, square at the bottom where they grew from under the skin. "Yes."

He held her hand in both of his. "It bothers me, too, but more abstractly. I don't particularly want a baby. But an older child—a son or daughter, nine or ten years old . . . To take to the aquarium on Sunday mornings. We'd watch the seals and talk about tropical fish in little tanks. The florescent yellow and purple ones. I love aquariums." He tickled the palm of her hand. "Sometimes I think, I've made love thousands of times, but it never worked. I never let it. Never tried. For all I know, I could be infertile." Stretching a piece of grass over his thumbs, he attempted to make a whistle. "But for me, the loss is acceptable. I love Marge—I can't imagine being married to anyone else any more than I can picture her as a mother. She's simply not maternal. So, it's a sacrifice I'm willing to make."

Ida looked at the rusty hills. "I thought it was irrevocable, that I'd have to appropriate a terrible injustice. But I can't get away from it. That gaping hole in my life, I just stand in front of it, paralyzed."

5

"Watch your step. Have a nice holiday."

Rose and Ida walked off the plane into the jetway. The humid air enveloped them as though they were entering a great, yawning mouth.

"How do they celebrate Thanksgiving down here without the frost on the pumpkin?" Rose shifted her flight bag to her other shoulder.

Ida searched for the baggage claim checks. "Florida is timeless—no planting, no harvest, no cold to endure. No spring, either."

"Ida, you always exaggerate!"

"Well, of course." She adopted a deep, professorial tone. "Exaggeration in the service of magnification. It helps you see what you'd otherwise miss."

Their suitcases were already riding round and round on the circular belt. "I'm surprised, Ida, that no one could manage to meet us. Your in-laws generally seem so solicitous."

"Oh, they are. But Max plays golf in the afternoon, and Bea goes to the hairdresser at two every Wednesday. Doris is timid about driving anywhere unfamiliar by herself."

"But surely the airport isn't unfamiliar. I'd imagine people come to visit now and then, and doesn't Doris ever travel up north any more?"

Ida pictured Doris as she usually stood, on one foot like

a crane, in a yellow wraparound skirt. With triangular pockets. "Not really, Rose."

They squinted from the white light reflected off the highway. The honeycomb compartments of condominiums, ribbed with outside porches, guarded the road. Rose put on her sunglasses. "I can't wait to taste those cool, salty waves."

The cab turned onto Hallandale Beach Boulevard. "You'll have to. They're not directly on the beach. But they do have a pool."

Max was standing just inside the rotunda with his golf buddies. Ida recognized him from his stance even before she was close enough to see his face. Leaning back, his center of gravity well behind his paunch billowing over plaid Bermuda shorts. And high white socks with white shoes, shiny clean.

"There's Ida, my daughter-in-law. Ida, Ida!" Max walked quickly with his toes pointing outward, each foot trying to get away from the other. "Don't try to lift anything." He kissed her on the cheek and looked away. "Hello, Rose. How are you?"

Bea was not at the hairdresser's since Mrs. Berger had an emergency and needed to be squeezed in at eleven. "Mother's in the pool. Swimming laps to gain weight." Ida and Rose spotted Bea in her white bathing cap with plastic flowers. Rolling her head from side to side, elbows bent, hands arched back at the wrist. "No more liquid protein and milk shakes. Just laps. Bea, Bea, the children are here.

Bea! Every day like this, back and forth, back and forth. Fifty laps in the shallow end. Bea!" Slowly, concentrating on her breathing. She couldn't hear the chorus of women sitting around the pool. "Bea, Bea. Max is calling you."

Up in the apartment Bea served ice tea and cake. "You girls must be tired from your flight. Sit down and rest. Doris should be here any moment."

Rose excused herself to unpack and shower. Bea put away the sugar and started to wipe the counter. "We got this new Formica. They said buff black is the latest thing, but every little speck of dirt shows. Still, it's wonderful—no borders around the edge where crumbs get stuck." The sponge left a trail of wet swirls. A string of glistening cursive *e*'s. Mrs. Weiss began to cry.

"Oh, Mother, it will be all right." Ida got up from the table and put her arm around Bea. "It hurts now, but we'll all heal."

Bea blew her nose in a sheet of decorator tissue from the flowered box on top of the dishwasher. "You know, Max invited Rob down for this weekend, but . . ."

"Oh, my God."

"Well, I told him he shouldn't do it without consulting you, but anyway Rob wouldn't come without *her*, and of course we couldn't have all three of you here, so it fell through."

Ida thought of Rob at the door, with a suitcase and garment bag. Standing in the foyer below his graduation picture, Bea's eyebrows on his face.

"Ida, Dad meant well. Don't be angry at him. He just thought you two would see each other again, and Rob would forget all about this other woman." She meshed her fingers, clicking together the rings from either hand. Back and forth. Back and forth. Clicking.

"Mom, you both have to get it out of your heads that this is something that will pass, like the flu. Rob has been seeing Sheila for two years now. We're not getting back together again."

Mr. Weiss walked into the kitchen. Bea turned toward the sink. "Here's your fruit, dear." Washing an apple and drying it carefully, "He just loves his fruit, he has an apple every afternoon. My good boy."

Max took it. "Ida, come here. Ida. Sit down, I want to talk to you."

"She's been sitting for hours. Let her stand if she wants."

"What?"

"I said, she's already been sitting too long!"

"Ida, I've been thinking. What do you need that job in Boston for? What do you make, twenty thousand maybe? You'll come down here and stay with us . . ."

"Dad, listen. Nothing you can do will change Rob's mind. It's over. I'm not moving down here so you can try to trap your son . . . Besides, I love my work."

Max waved his hand in front of his face. It's over—the same phrase on the phone last week, from Rob. I wish I could beat some sense into that boy. Quiet, Bea, I know I'm shouting. So if you can't stand it, go in the other room! Robert, are you listening, Robert? Robert?

"What does a woman have to work for? Ida, about Rob, you're probably right, but an old man can still hope, no? What's wrong with him! With a beautiful wife like you . . . Bea, give me some tea. Ida, let me explain to you—I don't want to talk about Rob now. The hell with him! When

Doris first got divorced, I thought it was the end of the world . . ."

"Dad, please. Let's try not to talk about it. We'll get nowhere and just upset ourselves. There's nothing to say. Come, let's just spend a nice few days together."

Max put his hand on the table. A heavy arm that didn't taper for a wrist. "Wait, Ida. I was saying, when Doris got divorced I thought it was the end of the world, but then I read in the *Floridian*. There was a study—nearly half the marriages these days end in divorce. Half! And those Jewish boys, when they break up with their wives, they always go, you know where? To their mothers. So they can cook for them. Down here in Florida. You stay here awhile, those boys are sad and lonely, no one to keep house and take care of them. You'll find one right away! I don't even worry for Doris any more. It's just a matter of time. And if it takes you even two years to find one—within the first year of marriage, say, if he makes, let's suppose forty thousand, you'll already make up for not working."

"Oh, Dad!" On the counter, a tiny snapshot of herself smiled in its gilded frame. A picture from high school with short, curly hair.

"Won't you just consider it, Ida?" Bea clicked her rings as Ida shook her head.

"See, Max? I told you it was useless to even bring it up. Ida, dear, we don't want to upset you, particularly at a time like this. We just want what's best for you. You do understand, don't you?"

The doorbell rang. "Oh, Max, that must be Doris. Go open the door."

Max took Doris's shopping bags. "Looks like you bought out the whole store!"

Doris and Ida kissed. "Oh, Ida. It's so good to see you. How are you? You should have seen Burdines today. A regular zoo!" Doris went into the bedroom, Max in tow, to hang up the new clothes so they wouldn't wrinkle.

Bea sat in the chair Max left. "That girl, she's a real gem, my Doris. You know, she's so well organized, and what a house she keeps! She never once ran out of toilet paper, not once in two years, and no man around to help her and raising those two children all herself! I never would have thought she could do it."

Doris came into the kitchen. "Ida, dear, I'm so sorry. I know how you must feel."

With Max right behind her. "It's all your fault, Doris."

"My fault! I haven't seen my brother in nearly a year, not that the louse ever listens to me anyway."

Max began peeling a banana. "What I mean is, it's easier when you're not the first. Once his big sister did it, he must have thought it was okay."

Doris opened the refrigerator. "Good, Mom. I see you bought some diet Coke for me. Incidentally, where's Rose?"

"A doctor, no less. My Doris leaves a doctor with a good practice!"

Bea scooped the apple peels into the disposal. "The nice thing about stainless steel is how fast the sink dries."

Leaving the room, Doris motioned for Ida to follow. "Oh, Dad. We've all heard this one a thousand times. If you don't mind, we'll pass for now."

"But Ida, I can't tell you how bad I feel." Squinting. His wrinkled nose and thick lips bunching up to crowd the eyes. "If you'd only had children! Why wait, I used to say. Right? Why wait when . . ."

"Dad, I've told you before, it was *Rob* who never wanted children."

"What?"

"*Rob* didn't want a baby!"

"So what. You couldn't fool him? Once the children came, he'd get used to them."

"Dad, I wouldn't do that."

At the entrance to the living room Max stood in front of the glass liquor cabinet set in mirrors. "Yes, but what about you, Ida? Now it's too late. At least Doris got her kids out of it. And the alimony . . ."

Doris took Ida by the hand. "Come, let me show you the robe I picked up on sale. And Dad, when you bring Mom home from the beauty parlor, could you swing by and get the kids? Since they had no school today, they're over at Jessica's swimming at the pool."

He nodded. "If you really want to know what I think, it's all the fault of Women's Lib." From the kitchen the faucet sang a high note. Long, and trailing off before a hiccuped coda. Bea was running hot water to defrost tomorrow's turkey. "In my day, no one got divorced the way they do today. I mean, if somebody was crazy or something was *really* wrong, but . . . it would be like divorcing your mother, you know what I mean? The point is that she was *yours*. Women then were pretty much all the same—one a little nicer looking, maybe, one a little fatter, one complained more, but basically, you wouldn't have a reason to change one for another."

Mrs. Weiss dried her hands and steered him toward the door. "We'd better hurry or I'll be late for my appointment."

"But now, you have women who make a hundred thousand! It's a temptation. It isn't right."

"Come, darling. We'll talk to Ida later. You girls have a nice, relaxing time. We'll be home before six."

In the living room white vinyl chairs, puffy as marshmallows, squatted on pale green carpeting. Wall to wall. "Rose, good to see you. I just love your kimono." Above the coffee table a piece of fabric, stretched across a frame, trumpeted in red and yellow. Stylized poppies and daffodils stamped in a repeating pattern.

"They've been taking it pretty hard, I guess." From the table Ida picked up an old candy dish. Fine china veined with tiny cracks.

"It's been especially hard on Mom, I suspect, even though Dad's the one who can't stop talking about it."

"Why is it harder for your mother, Doris?" Rose was winding a toy clown that played a drum. When it stopped moving and clicked like a cricket, she turned it over and looked at the mechanism. "You need a washer for this, or something to keep the metal from rubbing."

Doris felt in the shag carpeting for the missing part. "Well, Mom has never admitted it in so many words, but I think she feels doubly betrayed. In a way, Rob rejected us by always choosing women who were nothing like us. I hope you won't take this wrong, Ida, but at first we felt a little like that about you. A professional woman and all. In our house—how can I put it, men *do* the doing. Women just *are*."

"Oh, Doris, you make a home, shop and cook . . . How can you say you don't do anything?"

Doris found some barrettes along with the washer. "Of course, but that's not the point. Anyway, you were a shock until we got to know you." To Rose, "Our whole family's just *mad* about Ida! We made an exception. Or maybe not, come to think of it. A teacher—well, if you ask me, it's a different way of raising children, really, so even a college teacher isn't so far out of line. But now, a wealthy lawyer and a non-Jew!"

Rose walked over to the floor-length curtains. "Can I open these, do you think?"

"Oh, sure. It's late enough now—the sun won't fade the rug."

Below, shuffleboard courts and lounge chairs decorated the deck. Rose kept two hands on the curtain pull, her left going up as her right came down. "About the *doing* business. When I was growing up, I can't say I appreciated my mother very much. Or my aunts either, for that matter. The men held jobs—when they did. But we never saw their work. It wasn't *theirs,* if you know what I mean. Nothing of them in it, for all we knew. But what women did—take my mother, she could make perfect pie shells. Made them for everyone. Or Aunt Flo arranged flowers. As well as any professional florist. What the women did, even though they didn't make money—well, it was a specialty. Whether we recognized it or not."

"Not in our family. Naturally, Mother does some things better than I do, and vice versa, but we don't dwell on it. Personally, I find housework drudgery. At least I'm honest about it."

Rose looked down at the pool where a lifeguard watched a single swimmer. "So why did you choose that life for yourself?"

"Oh, don't get me wrong. I adore my freedom. You know, in college I was miserable most of the time. I hated doing papers and worrying about subjects I'd never use, like trigonometry or philosophy. I was petrified of being called on in class." Doris locked her hands behind her head. "Ida and I once talked about how she dreads interviews. Well, I'll never have to go to one, be scrutinized by a bunch of pompous asses. Who needs it? I can live without all that anxiety! They don't give awards for it, but I'm happy."

Awards. Mildred kept stacks of them in a Lord and Taylor box up the attic. Good attendance, perfect attendance, moderate achievement, excellence. From the Sunday School annual assembly, care of the Temple Sisterhood. Something for everyone, the rabbi intoning with florid flourishes. Ida remembered him on the pulpit: "We hope the recipients, these fine boys and girls, will go on to a long life rich in accomplishment. Learning, success, good deeds, *mitzvot*." Bombastic, Ida used to think, with her vocabulary word from the PSATs.

"From what Ida tells me, Rob too wanted more *being*, so to speak. I saw it myself whenever I visited—how he resented financial pressures, and the office."

The hated job at the *Post*. Ida remembered the headaches, and wet towels over his eyes. "Grape juice, he used to say. His code word for it. Spilling it out like grape juice when it could have been fine wine. He needed to let his thoughts sit." Now he can afford to stay home, with Sheila for a 'husband.' He can write all day and cook Chicken Kiev.

On the cocktail table were pictures of Rob on his tricycle. In a sailor suit. In a high chair. In black and white. Doris's children were in color shots. "If we want to get any sun today, we'd better go down now." Ida stood up. "Before they get back with the children."

"Sure."

In the hallway, the elevator hummed from below. The

metal doors rattled. "I was wondering, Ida, if you'd thought about your name. After Marvin and I split up, I did think about the question, but I wanted the same name as the kids, so that settled it. I stuck with Klein. Do you call yourself Weiss any more or Morgan-Weiss, or are you going back to Morgan?"

Ida shook her head. "Do you ever go back to anything, I wonder? I don't know, Doris. I really don't."

6

Snow in November. An early snow. Her first day back. Ida stood in the front vestibule watching it fall on the road. Big, wet flakes already starting to stick. The initial classes after the first school holiday were always difficult—trying to rekindle the excitement of learning, the pace of inquiry, the urgency of intellect on a bed of stuffing drenched in gravy. With the day's teaching behind her, Ida felt tired. Outside, a jogger trudged by in soggy sneakers that left a trail of melting question marks. All that slush between her and the warm living room where Rose was waiting with an answer.

Stepping outside the heavy glass doors, Ida caught the first clean whiff of winter, the cold promise of blanketed streets and aching wrists at the edge of mittens. Headlights cut the darkness with cones of swirling flakes. In her assigned space, Ida's green Ford slept beneath a thin sheet, dozing under its downy coverlet. A pity to disturb it. "I'll walk home."

She had always loved snow. Sledding in the deep powder on Glenny Hill, and crouching under the spruces that bent down to the ground with their white weight. Snug, enclosed, hidden, guarded. Panting. And indoors, silent night through the cold, black window with comforting, alien songs of a fatherless baby, a mother and child. Colored candles flickering in a row and houses lined in blue bulbs, or all in green.

She stopped on the B.U. bridge. Beyond the towers of the Law Library, the Prudential Building presided over blocky structures. The gold dome of the State House was barely visible—a precious gem braced in a setting of steel. Ida leaned over the railing toward the dark water tinged with red lights. Like glistening streaks of blood. Behind her a fence of iron girders, painted green, kept back the traffic.

Rose had slept a lot in Florida. Riding the bus last night, on the way home from the airport, she felt light-headed. Not dizzy, she said, but insubstantial—her feet relieved of all that weight. A touch of helium. In ten days a home test could sometimes tell, but Rose had delayed an entire month. Tonight, together in their own home, they would wait for a sign: a coded, chemical message.

From the bridge, a glittering fairyland. White petals clung to Ida's coat. She felt the prickle of sleet around her eyes.

"I need time. I'm still in mourning for Rob. My job is still new, my apartment, this city."

Like an echo off the water, "There is no more time. Only the wrong time or no time. Ready is too late."

Ida thought of her niece and nephew. They usually spent Christmas vacation with her; she looked forward to their coming every year. So did Doris. Last December there had been a surprise snowstorm in Washington. They had all gone tobogganing in Rock Creek Park.

"I've wanted it for years. I must not surrender more than I can bear to lose."

And her own sister, holding little Arthur. Ida swallowing again and again. Or mothers in the supermarket, their babies in infant seats. Bigger children sprawling out of shopping carts, buried in boxes of Tide and canned tuna fish. Telling them over and over again to sit down.

"I could find a father later."

A truck honked. A stalled motor whined repeatedly, trying to turn over. The road was icy. Rose would be expecting her.

What would her mother say, or Tom Martin, or the dean? Or Aunt Grace? Would she fail to be re-hired 'for budgetary reasons' unrelated to her teaching? She could move to another campus somewhere. Divorced, widowed, separated—the acceptable ways to be out of wedlock. Absent fathers, dead fathers, abusive fathers. And those in the army. All gone, invisible.

Wet feet. There was a temporary lull in the traffic. Again the snowy enchantment. Ida lowered herself beneath the frozen veneer, beneath prudence and fear, the concern of relatives, the gossip in the office of the registrar.

"Ida, Ida," from under the ice. "Say yes to yourself. To life." She stared into the opaque water. "For a blessing." Walking slowly down toward Brookline Street, she was limping. One foot had gone to sleep in the cold.

There was a pay phone outside the First United Market, a small, ethnic establishment struggling to stay in business. Ida was worried about Rose. Of all nights to be late! The lights from the grocer's front door poured out upon the snow. The phone was mounted on the brick wall.

"Hello, Rose? I'm so sorry it's taken me this long." A white lie—"Some trouble with the car." Ida missed all of Rose's words while listening to the tenor of her voice. Instantly she knew. "Yes, at the First United. I'll be home in a few minutes."

Ida stepped inside the store to dry off. On the floor along the counter was a row of amaryllis, white as lilies, growing in clay pots.

The proprietor smiled. "They force them in greenhouses to make blooming in winter. Very nice this time of year. Only five dollars. I wrap it up good in plastic for you."

"Thank you, yes, I'll take one." She left with the flowers under her arm.

Ida watched her feet as she walked. When she looked up, it was just a spot opposite her way down the road. It grew bigger. A jolly snowman in a rust red scarf. Closer. It was Rose. She looked at the flowers Ida carried. They embraced. They cried. Hugging, the two women danced in a circle under the street lamp.

"Can you really believe it, Rose?"

"I couldn't wait, I'm sorry. And then when it got late, and you still didn't arrive, I went to the pharmacy and spent another ten dollars on a second E.P.T. kit and did the test again! There's no doubt. I even threw up for good measure."

"Oh, Rose. But I mean, do you *believe* it?" Arm in arm they started back.

"The way I believe in God. A preposterous notion you hold for good reason in the absence of credible proof."

The street was empty now. They walked down the middle of the road, leaving footprints. Rose began to sing, and Ida took the alto part.

> God rest ye merry gentlemen,
> Let nothing you dismay

Rose broke into la's so as not to offend Ida. Their voices grew louder as they found the proper harmony, the tune ringing in the dry cold. The snow had stopped.

> O-oh, tidings of co-omfort and joy,
> Comfort and joy,
> O-oh, ti-idings of co-omfort and joy.

The gray paint was peeling on the outside door to his apartment, and the mailbox was loose. It hung down at an angle. Ida rang the bell and waited. No buzzer to open the lock, no intercom. No security system.

The knob turned one way and then the other before the door pulled back. Phil was wearing an apron tied above his waist. The smell of basil and sage followed him down the hall. Bowing low, a white dish towel draped over his arm, "*Entrez Madame. Le chef de la maison vous attend.*"

The inner door opened on the kitchen. Copper pots that were too pink dangled by their handles from mounted pegboard. A hemp throw rug, a framed photograph of sand dunes, blue napkins and matching candles on a blond wood table. The brick floor reminded Ida of the kitchenettes photographed with wide-angle lenses for *Better Homes and Gardens*. "And *I* welcome you too." He helped her off with her coat and kissed her. Craning his neck over her shoulder from behind and staying a little too long. When he pulled back, his lower lip stuck to hers.

Wine and cheese in the living room, jazz from the stereo. "So, Ida, tell me more about the kid who cheated on his term paper. Did he finally admit it?" And the antics of the assistant dean between crackers with sesame seeds. Over dinner, Phil asked about Rose.

"Do you really think she'll be able to raise a child alone?" He boned the fish while eating it, and kept the fork in his left hand.

"She's not alone. She has me. But even if she were, yes. Her own mother, who was infinitely less capable—financially, emotionally—raised four girls. Mostly without a husband."

Phil had prepared a flaming dessert. "To symbolize the kindling of passion, my dear."

"Ah, or the inferno of life."

"The conflagration of communion!"

"The fire of fear!"

"Fear? Nonsense. It's perfectly safe—at the first sign of trouble, we reach for the water glasses." A flicker of blue, and seven more matches. "These things never light in real life. Only in movies." Leaning forward, they ate together from the serving plate. "Anyhow, it's better this way. Why burn off all the booze?" After it got soupy, they switched to spoons. "Still, without a father—*ever*, I mean—don't you think there's something missing, fundamentally? Biologically?"

"What biology? Science gave you guys fatherhood. In a state of nature, men don't even know who their children are."

"Well, culture gave us fatherhood before science."

Ida dipped the end of her napkin in the water and rubbed at the syrup she'd dripped on her skirt. "By owning women, you could recognize your children—but still, a man is *told* he's a father. He never knows for sure. Fatherhood is an idea for men, a concept. Ideas come and go."

"While mothers, I take it, hang around."

They cleared the table. He washed and she dried. "So, Professor, are you deprecating the power of the mind as compared to the body?" He took back the saucer he'd handed her since it was still soapy on the bottom.

"On the contrary. I'm extolling the mind. Take me, for instance. I was adopted, my sister wasn't. But my father loved me as a daughter just as much as he loved Pearl.

Maybe more." She bunched up the towel and twisted it around to reach the bottom of the glass.

"And your mother?"

"Well, Pearl is temperamentally more like my mother than I am. But that's not entirely a matter of heredity—some children don't rebel, others do."

"And some are mutants. Let's not forget mutants."

"Thanks a lot! But short of mutation, there are just good old recessive genes."

"That's true, short mutants are definitely recessed."

"Oh Phil!" Ida put away the last piece of flatware. "I was thinking of Kafka, for example."

"And I was thinking of you. But speaking of recess, how about some cognac in the living room?"

The couch was a huddle of pillows crouched between giant bookends of oak. Ida sank down in the middle, Phil at the end.

"Put up your feet, my darling, and tell me all about it." Phil feigned a German accent. Taking her foot in his hands, he kneaded the toes. "And how about you, Ida? Thinking of Rose's baby with its secret father, do you wonder about the mother who was kept a secret from you? The woman who gave birth to you?"

"I think about lineage, of having a past to trace."

"Rose has taken the next step—from an unknown father to an unknowable one."

Ida made the liquor spin around in her glass, edging upward the faster it went. "I don't know how much it matters."

His hands became still on her feet. Another record dropped down on the stereo. A lilting tune without words from the Swingle Singers. Doo-be-doo-be-doo-be-doo-be. Mozart sung by bees.

"Will it matter to *your* baby?"

She pulled back one foot and tucked it under the other. "*My* baby!"

"Or have we been talking about *Rose* all night? I don't even know Rose. It's you I care about."

"And even if . . . What right would you have to ask me . . ."

"No right, Ida. Believe me. No right. Only concern." Running his thumb down the sole of the foot that was still extended. He cupped her heel. "And if I loved you?"

The needle was stuck at the end of the record, rhythmically crackling. Sollup, sollup, solup, solup. On the hassock, a box top from a puzzle held a few lines of blue edging fitted together. Gray pieces, upside down, were scattered right beside and on the floor.

"But Phil? Have we known each other three months? What have we had, five real dates?"

"I guess we shouldn't count the false ones, then. Like all the mornings I waited for you to get to school. Why the hell are you always late? And all the lunches. But those weren't *dates*, anyway. Right?" He dropped some of the pieces back in the box. "So, what does love take—ten dates? Twenty?"

"Phil . . ."

"No, don't say it. Listen. There's so much I don't know about you. Of course. I'd be a fool to pretend otherwise. But it's like the genetic code. Since we're onto genes tonight. Each gene is found in every cell. As different as the parts are—eyes, foot, hair, heart—dissect them far enough and it's all the same, the personal melody. I could hear the tune the third time I was with you, the same as the fifth. Yours."

He felt the words vibrate in his hands on either side of her face. "But it's too soon."

"I know that. What shall we do? Freeze-dry it and add the water later?"

Sollup, sollup, solup. He walked to the record player and pushed the reject. "Ida, stay with me tonight. I know it's too soon. You know I know."

She held the hem of her skirt and wrinkled it back and forth. Looking down. "It feels like a leap of faith."

"The body is a bridge."

"But for me, what I've known is a covenant." Folding the hem over double. "In all my life, only Rob. I have no . . . fluency." She stared at the molding that crossed the black window pane. On the other side, arteries of water wriggled their way down the glass. The wind sounded like the roar of drops against a shower curtain.

"Ida, it will be now or then. But only if it feels right to you. We can hallow tonight and each other now."

The pounding in her temples keeping time. When he lifted her in his arms, she still hadn't decided. One hand grasped her other behind his neck. "It's okay, Ida. I won't drop you."

The top left drawer of Ida's desk was brimming with papers. A disheveled stack of student pronouncements, awkward attempts at hide-and-seek. The stapled, the clipped, the folded and torn, those fastened under plastic or ripped from notebooks; loose pages written by hand and typed releases from word processors. Slowly they made their pilgrimage to the second drawer, beleaguered with garlands of red ink. Ida removed a few unmarked compositions to take home in her briefcase—three a day, like multivitamins. Careful not to overdose. But then she decided to correct one before leaving the office.

> I chose to compare Tolstoy's *The Death of Ivan Ilych*, James' *The Beast in the Jungle*, and Sartre's "The Wall" because I noticed that in all three works the main characters come to reappraise their lives in view of death.

Ida scrawled in the margin: Avoid the first person—keep the focus off yourself. In good writing the author is invisible—his message unobstructed by his presence. Try this: "All three works depict confrontations with death that occasion reappraisals of life."

> In Tolstoy's novel, death helps the main character to see the importance of love and realize the triviality of bureaucratic promotions, the worthlessness of materialism, and how vacuous all social conventions are.

Parallel construction—substitute "the vacuity of social conventions."

> Likewise, in *The Beast in the Jungle* John Marcher only

> discovers that he has squandered his opportunity for love and marriage after his lifelong girlfriend dies. The last name *Marcher* is ironically symbolic of this man's failure to "march," to act boldly in life instead of waiting passively for meaning and purpose to leap out at him.

Excellent point. Fine interpretation of the name!

> Sartre's "The Wall" is more oppressive than the first two novels because here love and devotion are devalued by death. How can this view of life be resolved with the outlook that death enhances love and the importance of generating life? Which perspective is ultimately right?

Perhaps, Steven, there are various "right" answers for different people. Truth may be polyphonic. Ida crammed more comments into the margins on the next page. Comma splice, wordiness, don't end sentences with prepositions, vary vocabulary, agreement, use the conditional tense.

> Death is life's frame, which helps put the parts of the painting into some kind of perspective. It alters our view of time and makes us conscious of history. Personal discontinuity demands, at the very least, a renewed estimation of those experiences that span individual annihilation.

Beautiful, Steve. In the face of death, those links that tie the self to others can be affirmed as the only salvation from isolated finitude, or they can be ridiculed for their fragility in the wake of death's negation. The alternative depends on philosophical analysis but also on moral judgment, on personal courage, as Tolstoy suggests. A good ending to a fine paper! Watch out for mixed metaphors.

Rose pulled back the couch and began vacuuming the baseboard behind it. With one hand on the bookshelf to steady herself, Ida climbed down from the stepladder.

"Rose, maybe I should do that and you dust. Here, take the Pledge."

"Uhuh, and in a couple of months neither of us will be able to vacuum, right? The next thing you know your boyfriend or stud, or whatever, will have to come over and take out the garbage for us every day!"

"Rose!"

"I'm sorry, I shouldn't have said that. All I meant was, the baby isn't rattling around in there. It won't become detached when I lean over or lift something. Just relax, will you?"

Ida straightened the magazines on the coffee table while Rose started washing the windows. Ammonia squeaking in two keys—high and low. One of Magritte's room-sized apples screamed from the cover of a journal Ida hadn't had a chance to read. She flipped through the pages. Huge rocks on the ground or suspended in midair. Better drop the subject—that wasn't Rose talking, anyway. If it made her vomit when it was still a pimple, by now it could make her roar. And mornings are especially difficult.

"Rose, are you sure you don't want to come along to Connecticut? I'd really like to have you with me, if you felt up to it, and you'd be able to get to know Phil."

"No, thanks. You two run along. I'll just spend a quiet day catching up on some reading."

Ida rolled the end of her rag and tried to get at the dirt

between the grooves on the television speaker. "You don't like him, do you? What have I said that makes you think badly of him?"

"I have nothing against him personally. He's probably a nice enough man. It's *you* I'm concerned about." Rose loudly crumpled some papers lying on the desk. "I can't figure out what you need this for. You've just gotten over a disastrous relationship—"

"No, Rose, it wasn't *disastrous*. It had many beautiful parts. That's why losing it hurts."

"In any case, since you've asked my opinion, I just feel that if you had any sense you'd stay away from men for a while. Give yourself time to get back on your feet before putting yourself in jeopardy again. You should take this chance to revolve around your own center for a change, instead of serving somebody else's needs. Why complicate your life? And what can this man really give you, Ida? A married man with his own agenda? Of course, I can see what you're giving him!"

Sitting down in the rocking chair. Slowly, with spaces between the words, "Nothing he's not giving me, Rose. People do that together, you know."

"I wonder." She wiped a long-necked vase and put it back between a dictionary and the parisian elephant.

"Rose, sit down for a minute. This is important to me. That you hear me." Balancing the can of spray wax on the radiator, "I complicate my life because I'm not simple in the first place. Yes, he's married, in a peculiar enough way, I suppose, but I'm not looking to get married tomorrow, either. And if I do remarry, I expect it will be to a Jewish man. You know that matters to me. Anyhow, to be centered—that's the prerequisite, like in pottery, but it's the extension out from the middle that makes the pot."

"Ida, I'm not saying you should become a hermit, but jumping into things so fast . . ."

"Sexually, you mean."

"Well, yes, to be blunt." She leaned over to pick a loose piece of thread from her sock.

Ida pictured Phil braced on his forearms, looking down at her. With big, wet eyes and short lashes. Moving inside her, his head held still. And lying on their backs eating potato chips in bed. Where could you fit these scenes in an album of limericks and pornographic postcards?

"Rose, I'm not 'fooling around,' if that's what you think. Taking off your clothes with someone—forget intercourse now—just sharing each other's nakedness, it's seeing another person and being seen. Revelation comes in revealing. For me, it's something holy and intimate. An affirmation."

"You want me to condone it? I can't." She stared at the fireplace next to Ida.

"I know *you* can't. But you must understand that I'm *me*, not you. I'm not leaving you, or the baby, to live with him—you know that, don't you? Know it. But also, to appreciate something is not only to recognize its worth but to enhance it. And vice versa."

"So now I'm ruining your 'holy communion' if I don't embrace it with open arms. If you really felt right about this, you wouldn't need my blessing."

Her father's blessing. Each Sabbath, his hands on her head. First Ida, then Pearl. "Rose, what can I say? A blessing isn't an embrace. You hold your hands out straight on someone else's head—at arms' length."

Rose stood up and removed from the mantelpiece a glass with some soda in the bottom. The glass had stuck to the wood. "Why must you leave this stuff around?" She scratched with her fingernail at the ring left underneath.

"Ida, I'll meet him today when he comes to pick you up, before he drives with you on this journey you're going on, or whatever it is. God knows if you'll find what you're looking for, so you can get back to being yourself here . . . Anyway, if I can't manage a blessing, perhaps a plenary indulgence?"

"Whatever that may be, it's something. Thanks, Rose."

"Well, we may have cleared the air a little, but the floor is still a mess! You mop the linoleum and I'll finish the rug in here, unless you want him to trip over the electric broom when he arrives!"

Ida looked at her watch. "Shit, he'll be here in ten minutes. And my luck, he'll be right on time!"

After passing M.I.T., they turned right at Memorial Drive. The river ran along the left. Ida unbuttoned the top of her coat as the heater began to work. Phil opened his window a crack. "Just a precaution—this sporty old cruiser is older than I like to admit." He lit a cigarette and inhaled slowly. "Rose was quite cordial when we met."

"Did you expect her to throw a pot at you?"

"No, but there was less hostility than you'd described. She was guarded but somehow not, well, I don't know how to put it." The smoke seeped out of his mouth and wandered around his cheeks.

Ida thought about the ticket machine on the Mass. Pike and then the Sturbridge exit. And the last leg of the trip back. She was getting ahead of herself. "Actually, we spoke about it just before you came. Maybe that helped." Dreamily.

Phil tossed a quarter into the toll basket and switched on the radio, turning the volume down low while humming to himself. A trailing melodic line that ended where it began.

The windshield was dirty. Ida stared at the haphazard stains; the background beyond it blurred. Had anyone ever told her not to ask? Was anything explicitly proscribed? Actually, she'd known about it all her life. No tricks, no stigma. Only thankfulness, acceptance, wonder. What began as a curse for some nameless, helpless girl, was miraculously transformed into a blessing for a childless couple. "Today, I might have been an abortion," she thought.

A squirt of fluid and the wipers took away the stain. Ida looked at Phil's profile, a soft mouth between the angles of nose and chin. His neck muscles showed beneath smooth baby skin. A touching incongruity. "I really appreciate your coming with me. And juggling your classes around to get off. You didn't have to, you know."

"*Have to*? If it's obligatory, it's not a gift. And I'm glad you wanted me along on something like this." Rocking her knee with his hand, "What are you really looking for, Ida? What do you want to find?"

Not lost and found, for she'd never been lost. Not new parents—parents she had. But ancestry—not just proximity. To be connected with humanity, the thread leading all the way back. And the cross-weave: relatives. To be knit into the fabric of life, like normal people. Instead of hovering above the cloth.

"Maybe this thing is all in your head."

"Maybe. But I have to know, Phil, if it matters. How much it matters. Before I decide for my child. As long as I have a choice, I need to know." Sperm banks and multiple donors. Ida pictured rows of test tubes, running over the top.

"Do you know anything about your real parents?"

"Only that both were Jewish. The agency told my parents that."

He tried to imagine himself adopted. Without his father's hairline and Uncle Jack's flat feet. "Do you think if you hadn't considered artificial insemination, that you'd be searching for your past?"

"I don't know. Maybe it would have been enough to realize I could if I ever needed to. Like if I developed a hereditary disease or needed medical information. Or a relative's kidney."

"Hey, Ida. That could make a great book. How about a series? *In Search of the Lost Kidney—An Ida Weiss Mystery*."

"Sure. It could be very modern. *Ida Weiss in Caracas, Lost in the Aleutians, Doubles for Divorce*. Fast moving, action packed."

"*Mass Mobility and the Missing Microbe, The Technological Twins*."

"People wouldn't like it, though. You need something with a clear moral. That biblical touch. The sequel could read: *Beware the Will of God* or *Who Maketh the Barren Woman a Happy Mother of Children*."

"Uhn uh. Too long. Something short and snappy, like *For Better or Worse*." He checked the number of the exit as it passed by. "Where the hell are we? You're supposed to be telling me where to get off."

"Hold your horses. We're not there yet."

Phil turned the radio dial in search of a local station. Then he pointed his chin from side to side. "My neck always gets stiff on long car rides." Switching to the right-hand lane, "This fellow we're staying with tonight, who is he?"

"I know him from high school. Arnie Capella. Last week I remembered that he was involved with some kind of adoptee organization. He's made some calls for me and says he can help us. He's a nice guy. You'll like him."

"Did you two date back then?"

"What is that I see creeping onto the dashboard? Jealousy?" Melodramatically, "A hot romance, cooling over twenty-odd years!" Ida laughed. "To tell you the truth, he used to go out with a friend of mine."

They found a parking space on Trinity Street within sight of the Capitol, its gold dome shining against a blotter of clouds. Then down the incline toward Elm Street. The Department of Health, set beside the Family Court, was only a few blocks away. Across the street tall trees lined their namesake, but on the other side, near the government offices, nothing grew.

A federalist structure with a blue and gold mosaic, nonfigurative: the Health Department. A dog pound for secrets. Go to the second floor, Arnie had said. The Bureau of Vital Statistics.

Statistics—a word with sharp edges. A ticking sound with hisses. Statistics, like dead shells. Hard, cold, inorganic. Only viable when joined with their makers. Only vital to the creatures that produced them. Ida's heels clattered on the outside steps.

They rode the elevator together. Then Phil waited for her in the hallway.

Behind the counter, Ida shifted her weight from one foot to another. A secretary, studying a computer printout, stood on the other side.

"Excuse me. Can you help me? I'd like a copy of my birth certificate."

"Certainly, I'll bring you a form to fill out."

"Thank you. I need my original birth certificate, the unamended version."

"Pardon me?"

"I was adopted. I'd like to see . . ."

"Oh, I see, but you're not entitled to your documents, in that case."

As Arnie had scripted it for her, "Yes I am. The law in Connecticut currently allows adoptees to obtain their original birth certificates."

"I'm sorry, Miss. I've been instructed not to give adopted children any sealed records."

"Obviously, I'm not a child. May I speak to your supervisor, please."

Ida was led to a large room that held an armored division of desks. Metal, evenly spaced, identical. Immaculate. Closest to the door one desk supported an electric pencil sharpener and a cork globe with yellow pencils sticking out of it—all with perfect points. A porcupine to guard the appointment calendar and letter opener. A woman in a straight, navy skirt and white blouse sat behind her tank. "Yes?" Ida repeated the request.

"I'm very sorry, but such inquiries must be submitted in writing three weeks in advance." Her frosted hair was in ringlets.

"But I wasn't told that when I called last week."

"Do you know whom you spoke to?" Of course, Ida didn't. "Then I'm afraid there's nothing I can do for you now." The woman removed her tortoiseshell glasses, which hung around her neck on a chain.

"Over the phone I was informed that I must come to Hartford in person. I drove two hours to get here, and now you're telling me it must be done by mail. Can I have your name along with a written statement that my birth certificate will be sent to me upon receipt of a written request?"

"No, dear, you can't." Barely moving her lips.

Arnie had told Ida that the office was in violation of

the law, stalling until new legislation would go into effect withholding original birth records from adoptees. "But according to the laws of this state, I'm entitled to a copy of my unamended birth certificate!"

"That may be the law, but it's not our procedure."

"You can't institute illegal procedures . . ."

"Miss, I'd like to help you, I really would. But I can't. If you'll excuse me, I have work to do." The woman returned her glasses to her nose and took an envelope from one of her drawers.

Back in the elevator, Phil fiddled with the zipper on the slim case of papers Arnie had sent to Ida as ammunition. "It's the arbitrary exercise of petty power. Bureaucracies are all the same."

"I should have said my name was Dr. Weiss. I wonder how many *children* are doctors?"

"While you were in there, I was reading some of the stuff Arnie gave you. Why do they always speak about the illegitimate child? Why not illegitimate parents? The *kid* didn't do anything wrong."

They walked beneath the portico down the front stairs. "The damn legislators! They hate women, is what it is."

"Now, Ida. Half the adoptees are *men*."

"Yes, but what do you think this whole thing is about, when a single woman gets pregnant? The whole hullabaloo. Not that she's had sex outside of marriage, not today, anyway. And not that the children might be raised without a father. If a woman is pregnant and her husband dies, they don't encourage her to give the child away, even though the baby will be just as fatherless. What's going on here is that unwed mothers are an assault on the male ego. How dare a woman take it upon herself to have a child without a man's consent or support!"

Phil checked the parking meter to see if it had run out. "Well, you don't even need our participation any more, right? What is it you told me that Rose's doctor said? Twenty billion sperm in a little milk carton, and frozen they last indefinitely. You can keep more than enough in your freezer for the entire population of the earth! Men are getting to be damn near superfluous!" He unlocked the passenger door. "Okay, Ida. What now?"

"I have an appointment with the probate judge at two o'clock. Those bastards on Elm Street may think they can do whatever they damn please, but this is still America!"

"Figuratively speaking."

"America?"

"No, bastards." He started the car, and they both began to laugh.

In operatic tenor, "God bless America, land that I . . ."

"Okay, Phil. Okay. Anything, but don't sing."

Main Street. The Municipal Building. Granite steps, brass railings, an enclosed atrium. A harlequin pattern in stone and glass, a spiral staircase, again the second floor. Ida leaned on the gray marble counter. "The judge will see you now. His chambers are on the left."

The office was lined with walnut veneer paneling and bookcases. Heavy volumes bound in maroon and black; gold lettering flecked from the bindings. Dark walls, with whitewashed plaster eight feet above. The window behind the judge's oak desk glared brightly. Ida shifted in her chair, trying to find an angle from which she could look at him without squinting. The venetian blinds cast horizontal bars across the room.

"What can I do for you, my dear?" Sandy brown hair, thinning. A face full of faded freckles.

"I understand that people can gain access to their adoption records for good cause. I would like to see my own file and therefore wish to know what constitutes 'good cause.' "

"May I ask how old you are?"

"Just thirty-nine."

"Ah. Are you married? Let me guess, you have teenagers at home. Have they left for college yet?"

Ida changed positions in her seat. She ran her thumb along the nailhead trim that studded the sides of her leather chair. "Your Honor, I don't have any children. Could you explain the grounds for obtaining records? Exactly what type of documents are maintained here?"

"Your name is Ida, isn't it? Tell me, Ida, do your parents know that you're meeting with me?"

"Sir, my father is dead, and—"

"Oh, I'm very sorry."

"My father died almost twenty-four years ago. Are psychological criteria part of the determination?"

"I bet your adopted mother would be terribly hurt if she knew you were trying to learn about your so-called 'natural mother.' Were your parents good to you? Out of respect for them, you should let this alone."

"Judge O'Connor, this doesn't have anything to do with my family. It's a search for my past."

"The past, young lady, is best left where it is. We all have to live in the present, right? You can't march into the future facing backward."

"Nor can you chart tomorrow's direction without knowing where you were yesterday."

On his desk a boat in a bottle was mounted on wooden bookends. He straightened the base so that the ship sailed toward a cubic digital clock. "Let me tell you a story, Ida, something I've always remembered and found instructive. Back when I was in college, I roomed with a young man who wanted to be an archaeologist. The chap studied all the time, a real scholar. But he was sort of a strange fellow. Antisocial. Had very few friends. I always felt that his obsession with the past was unhealthy. Regressive, I should say. Ours is the age of futurism—next year's cars come out a half year in advance, futures are traded on the commodity exchange. You have to be forward-looking today. Turn the pages, Ida, go on with your life."

"But don't you start at the beginning when you read a book?" This was not the way. If she won the argument, he'd surely harden his resistance. Ida felt queasy. She thought of Minute Man Park. The British regiment, all in a line, had been shot by the colonists hiding behind trees. She couldn't seem to duck behind the shrubbery.

"Your beginning, my darling, happened at the moment when they cut the cord and separated you forever from the past."

No. I began even before the slavery in Egypt. And back in the first commonwealth, in ancient Palestine. I can trace my origins to the Roman expulsion of the Jews to the four corners of the earth. I just need to know which corner. "Maybe the world needs archaeologists *and* judges."

"Just imagine, for a moment, this 'real mother' you're seeking—God only knows who the father may be, perhaps the woman herself wasn't sure. Anyway, picture this lady, in her later years now, sedate, content, passing her time in the bosom of her family, finally having rid herself of painful memories. Then you suddenly appear to remind her of a terrible chapter in her life. You shatter her dignity, her husband's trust, the innocence of her children."

From psychology to literature. The dime novel. Ida unfolded her hands. "We could just as well conceive of a woman who has always wondered what became of her child—if she had a good home, if she lives nearby. Were I that mother, I'd want to know—after twenty or thirty or forty years—that my daughter or son was well."

"But which mother is *really* out there, Ida? We have no way to know."

"And that's why we should rely on legality rather than fantasy. I have a right to my past."

"But the woman who gave birth to you has an absolute right to her privacy."

"As long as it doesn't violate someone else's rights."

"So you're telling me you need to know for psychological reasons."

"For legal reasons."

He placed the tips of his fingers together—thumb to thumb, index to index, pinky to pinky—as though caging an invisible ball. The warm-up position for the Eentsy Weentsy Spider. "A teenager came to me six months ago who had somehow gotten hold of hospital records indicating that her mother had taken diethylstilbestrol. This girl pleaded for her records to be opened in order to discover whether her mother took the drug *before* she was born, as well as after, since the risk of cancer is higher among the offspring of such users. I told her she'd live or die, in either case. I didn't consider *her* argument 'good cause,' and you expect me to honor some kind of vague need for mental peace?" He looked through the gaps between his fingers and saw the numbers dropping down on the clock. "My goodness, it's past three already!"

Ida hadn't slept much the night before nor had she eaten breakfast. Maybe there would be a ladies' room on the ground floor.

Phil was waiting by the elevator when she stepped out. "How did it go? You certainly must have gotten his attention—your meeting lasted nearly . . . Oh, Ida."

"Damn," drying her face with the back of her hand. "Let's get out of here." Back in the car, Phil jiggled the gears between forward and reverse. Trying for neutral.

"I hardly ever cry, you know." She looked for tissues in her pocketbook. "I can watch the saddest movies dry-eyed while everybody else is bawling." Somewhere between the judge's dismissal of the past and his creation of the imaginary mother Ida realized she might never find the answer. Seek and ye shall find—the haunting phrase. Bullshit. Seek and you're a seeker, that's all.

"Want a Milky Way? They had a candy machine in the basement and I . . ."

"No, thanks."

"How about the adoption agency?"

She shook her head. "I called them last week. They claim they can't find my records. That I could have come through another agency or that my parents lied to cover up a black-market adoption." Not after all those years studying Talmud every Saturday. All that legality and due process.

"Do you think that the agency could have lost your file?"

"Probably they're just not trying very hard to find it.

They may feel conflicted about the whole thing. Jewish law wouldn't favor secret name changes to disguise identity, either from fear of accidental incest or from a different attitude toward the past. Remember the genealogy of the begats?"

"One of Arnie's pamphlets gives a rundown of laws in other countries. I noticed that Israel releases records to both adult adoptees and birth parents." Phil wondered whether the agency might have filed Ida's records under the last name of the first mother or even under Ida's original name. "How about a break, Ida? Do you want some lunch?"

"I'd rather skip it for now, if that's all right with you. Arnie said to call him in the afternoon if we weren't successful. He has one more approach for us to try." While Ida found a phone booth, Phil warmed up the car. Then they headed back to Elm Street.

Snow had begun to fall, gusting across the road like swirls of dust, gathering in the gutters. Arnie was already waiting in his car beside a meter. He guarded a second parking spot for Phil and Ida. Phil pulled his Triumph into the free space.

Stepping out onto the sidewalk, Arnie stuffed his bare hands into shallow pockets. "Brrr. Well, here I am—your own personal, traveling notary public, at your service. How are you holding up?" They started back to the Health Department. "You've got those papers I gave you?" Phil lifted the briefcase in response. "Good, just checking. It always pays to be sure."

Again, at the counter on the second floor. "I'm sorry, Miss, but the woman you spoke to earlier, my supervisor, has left for the day. They're predicting quite a storm. All government offices may be closing early. You'll have to come back tomorrow—if we're open, depending on the depth of the snow—or possibly the next day."

"I can't. I have to get back to work in Boston. I've already taken off one day."

"Well, I'm very sorry, but there's really nothing . . ."

"Excuse me." Arnie laid the briefcase on the counter. "We're preparing to seek a writ of mandamus to enforce public duty. I'm a notary, and this gentleman is a witness." Arnie removed some documents. "We plan to serve papers on the most senior public servant now present in these offices. If you can find someone higher up to assume responsibility, fine. If not, we'll name you as the person who refused to give this woman a copy of her birth certificate, to which she is legally entitled according to the Connecticut statute reproduced here." Unfolding a photocopy of the legislation, "If you knowingly violate a law, you may have to answer for your actions in court."

The secretary pulled her hands off the counter as if it were the burner on a stove. "Just one moment, sir. I'll see if the assistant commissioner is still here. The commissioner himself has left already."

In the private office a stocky man, wearing a dark suit and striped tie, filled the swivel chair. His hands were folded on the desk. Just right for The Lord's Prayer before The Pledge of Allegiance. The secretary waited at the door. A young clerk hovered behind the deputy assistant commissioner.

Arnie stood stiffly, his heels together, like a soldier out

of *The Nutcracker Suite*. Ready to be wound up. "We have prepared an affidavit for you to sign indicating that on this day, the twelfth of December, at four o'clock in the afternoon, while acting in your official capacity, you denied the petitioner a copy of her original birth certificate."

The commissioner looked up from the papers. "Are you a lawyer?"

"No, sir, I'm not, but I have spoken to my attorney, and he has put himself at our disposal should we need him. If you would like, I can call him right now, and he could meet us here within—"

"Oh, no. That won't be necessary." For Christ's sake, we don't need any lawyers around here! "Miss Weiss, uh, Morgan-Weiss, do you know of any reason why you have been denied this certificate?"

Miraculously, from insurmountable complications to routine delivery. "No, not any reason that . . ." From the edge of the bookcase hung a paper wind chime of winged babies with bows and arrows. Ida stared at the red cutouts floating in the air. Not angels, not fairies . . . "Not any reason I can possibly think of why my rights should not be honored." Not cupids, those fat little . . .

The commissioner studied the documents a few more moments. Today of all days! Myrtle will probably be afraid to drive home from the real estate office. And I haven't had time to get the snowblower fixed. "Justin?" Turning to the clerk, "Would you please bring this woman a copy of the pertinent records."

Not angels, not seraphim. She fished for the word.

"Miss, let me apologize for any inconvenience we may have caused you. Things are not exactly normal around here today, with the weather and all. Surely you can understand. I don't know why you encountered any sort of problem. Perhaps the people who generally deal with these matters weren't here."

Putti! That's right, putti. In all those Italian frescoes with gilded sunbeams coming down from the sky.

"Miss Bartok, in light of the delay we caused Miss Weiss, we're going to waive the duplication and processing fees."

The clerk returned with a white, sealed envelope. Red putti danced in the moving air. Ida walked out of the office, between her bodyguards.

Arnie pushed the front door against the wind. "Congratulations, Ida. You're only the second applicant we know of who was able to get an unamended birth certificate from this place over the last year."

"How did the first one do it?" Phil hugged Ida, kissing the side of her forehead.

"He sat there every day for three weeks. They got sick of him."

She held the envelope with both hands, waiting to open it in the car.

Arnie molded a wet snowball and threw it at a passing taxi. "Now we know the secret of success! We've gotta wait until we catch them in a blizzard."

Certificate of birth, number 7448. Place of birth: St. Francis Hospital. But she had always thought it was Mount Sinai! Had she ever asked? Time of birth: 12:45 a.m. Twin or triplet? No. Length of mother's stay in hospital before delivery: 10 hrs. 5 mins. Five minutes? Who calculated her stay to the minute? Ida didn't even know what country her family came from, but now she knew the length of her mother's labor.

Full name of the child—in heavy capitals, crossed out but still legible through the lines typed over the letters: IDA GREENSPAN. Greenspan! She closed her eyes. "*Shehechiyanu*, Who has kept us in life and sustained us until this time. Blessed art Thou, oh Lord." Ida; the first name had never been changed. What's in a name? Nothing, her mother had said, when Ida dropped Morgan for Weiss and the new name pinched. Still nothing, ten years later, when she reasserted Morgan. But even Doris had asked this time. What's in a name? Why Israel instead of Jacob? Why Sarah and not Sarai? Or Avram renamed Abraham. A silly little extra syllable. Greenspan, from the mother who'd given life to her. Ida could not reach back across the ocean, but now she could see as far as her birth. With a name for it. Ida Greenspan. A beginning, her own *bereshit*. Does it matter how the world was created? Or when? If it took seven days or two millennia? Why give a time? There's no way back.

Above the large letters, squeezed in the blank: Ida May Morgan*. On the bottom of the next page, beside the asterisk, the date of the name change, executed at the Probate Court of Hartford more than a year after her birth.

Mother of child: Emily Greenspan. Age: 18. Birthplace: Bridgeport, Connecticut. Usual occupation: none. Place of occupation: none. Social security number: nothing.

Father of child: __________. Residency: blank. Race: blank. Age: blank. Birthplace: blank. Usual occupation: blank. Place of occupation: blank. Social security number: blank.

Other children previously born to this mother: 0. Now living: 0. Now dead: 0.

7

"Please put away all notes at this time, and deposit any bookbags or backpacks at the front of the auditorium." Shuffling, murmurs, the squeaky hinges of lap desks. "All right, quiet down now." Glancing at Pamela in the closest seat, "Now relax. If you've prepared properly, you'll do just fine. It's a fair test. No curve balls, no tricks." Walking up the aisles, Ida passed xeroxed papers down the rows. "Put your name on the midterm sheets themselves as well as on the blue examination booklets. Write legibly."

Raised hands. "Yes, I see that. For those of you who cannot read the second question—the duplication process must have been faulty—I'll rewrite that part on the blackboard." Ida began to copy the question on the board, her white letters with long strokes and full loops wandering across the green slate. In the absence of lines to sit on, the chalk marks set an undulating course.

> Compare the dramatic forms of tragedy and comedy with respect to plot, setting, characterization, dialogue, and philosophical orientation. Apply the dichotomy you develop to Euripides' *Iphigenia* and O'Neill's *Ah Wilderness*.

The whisper of lead points speaking to paper, the scrubbing of frantic erasers. A hand in the air.

"Yes, you must answer *all* of the essays."

Two full hours to patrol. Ida walked toward the middle

of the hall, picking up candy wrappers and balled pieces of paper left on the floor from the last testing period. Bryan Hastings was staring at the exit sign over the doorway. Rita Harrison was scribbling. Ida smiled at little Susan Anderson who was stroking a rabbit's foot. Dyed pink.

Ida made her first circle around the room, returning slowly to the front. She leaned against the podium. The students settled down, and Ida loosened the knotted muscles of her stomach. She remembered sleepless nights and hurried reviews from her own student days. Not behind her, those nights, but within. She looked at the clock. 12:45. The last day of the first semester.

Two weeks. For two weeks now she'd known her name. It still glowed. Early this morning when she first woke, she didn't know. Returning to the void for those foggy first moments. And then she remembered, and it was given to her again. To carry around as she dressed and prepared breakfast and gathered her work for school. And blossoming in her now; a deeply rooted, peaceful flower of knowledge with no purpose or use but its fragrance. She breathed deeply.

Another hand.

"No, Malcolm, you cannot substitute *Major Barbara*. If I'd wanted you to write about Shaw, I would have specified that play." A gifted student, but erratic. Ida recalled his insightful comment on dramatic irony. And his excessive absences.

For two weeks now: Ida Greenspan May Morgan-Weiss. Almost long enough for a character in a Russian novel! Too bad Mildred hadn't kept her maiden name, adding yet another suffix.

Ida sat down in one of the chairs at the back. St. Francis. Seven years ago in Assisi she'd walked around that monk's holy cliffs. The Italian mountainside he loved now hosted a great stone church, built to honor the humble ascetic who shunned rigid institutions. A simple love of nature, a quiet man of healing. But also the renunciation of material goods, the disparaging of family ties. Eight hundred years later, halfway around the world, a hospital bore his name. They sent her records upon request: Ida's own birth, as well as Emily's giving. More names. Morris and Ethel, grandparents, the third generation back.

Tom Martin entered through the swinging doors up front. He looked for Ida, then spotted her. Walking over, he sat down next to her in the empty seat. "I didn't see you at first. I thought you were one of the students."

"Ah, but I am."

He offered to spell her if she wanted to leave for a few minutes. Ida thanked him but declined. In hushed voices, "So, what are you doing over the vacation?" Tom would be skiing in Maine.

"I'll see you later in the faculty lounge."

Phil was going to California. To Marge. Of course, and Ida had always known it. But still. He would be leaving tomorrow. More than a month without him. Two weeks ago, teaching Hemingway's "Big Two-Hearted River"—she forgot him. Until the class was over. Like playing Monopoly as a child, when the game board stretched to the horizon of the mind—and then afterward, the world suddenly returning all around the edges: her mother, lunch, the bed she needed to make. The swing in the backyard, her bird eggs, the boxes of mica. The thrill that they'd all gone—the power of thought, of the game. And the bigger thrill, what came back. Phil. Tonight, in less than three hours. For dinner at the Voyager in Harvard Square. And after.

Barbara Firestein wanted to use the ladies' room. Security procedures—monitors, refusals, early exam submissions. "No, that's okay. Just go. But do hurry along." Ida rose, stretched, and began another circle of the hall. Over to the back aisle, down the left side, across the front, then up again. "May I have your attention. Half of the exam period is now over."

Last week she'd driven to Bridgeport. For an old yearbook in the town library. She found a face. A higher forehead, a different mouth, the eyes a little closer to the nose—but the same eyes. Ida's eyes. Smiling out from the pages. Beneath the picture: "Molly." A nickname. Oh Molly. The only relative Ida had ever seen. Pages later, Molly again. In the front row of the glee club. Short, curly-haired Molly, standing on the end, a bit behind the girl next to her. And at the back of the book was the school song: "Years So Dear" by Emily Greenspan. Ida xeroxed it. At home, Rose played the music on the piano. Like seeds found within Egyptian tombs, to provide sustenance for swaddled mummies. When the archaeologists planted them, they grew.

Ginger needed a second blue book. She dawdled at Ida's side. "Maybe, Professor, you could just tell me whether the answer I gave in section two is right?" Ida shook her head.

The boy beside her in glee club, an ungainly lad in glasses. Milton J. Flossenheim. Could there possibly be two? Only one Flossenheim in the phone book. Solomon Flossenheim. Ida called him. A brother. Milton had moved to New Jersey. But yes, he had known Emily Greenspan. A year younger in school. She married a boy from Israel and moved to a kibbutz. Who could forget, one of our own girls. When? Not sure. No, wait. The same year the family business failed. Yes.

A few students finished early and left. Alan Eagleton wanted to know if *equivocate* had two a's or two i's. More trips to the bathroom, pens that ran out, explanations of false starts and rewritten paragraphs. Reminders to sign your name.

"Start to finish up now. There are only five more minutes to the end of the test."

Ida watched the number of empty seats grow. She had never been to Israel. Didn't Aunt Grace have a cousin in Tel Aviv? Even if she didn't look for Molly. She could decide later. Otherwise, she'd have to go to Houston with her mother and visit Pearl and the baby. But how to explain such a sudden change of plans? Perhaps she could give a lecture at the Hebrew University or attend a conference? Some kind of last-minute opportunity. And Phil would be away.

"I'm sorry. Time's up. Jack, Esther, Horace. That's it."

They got up slowly, writing while walking. "Doctor Weiss, there's never enough time!"

"I know. You can't cover everything. But better than finishing is to make a good start."

"I couldn't remember, who painted *The Third of May*? Goya or Delacroix?"

"Does the term 'apostrophe' mean poetic address?"

"The Futurist painters advocated violence, speed, and the hatred of women, didn't they?"

"Who was Jean Paul Marat?"

Relief, exhilaration, disappointment, comradery. "Have a nice vacation, Dr. Morgan."

"And you too, my friends. You, too."

part two

8

El Al. To On. Upon. The prepositional airline. No wonder they never translate it. Little words that give location or direction. Hours in the sky bridging hurried connections. Ida looked down at the ocean, at boats and breakers reduced to ellipses. White blemishes on the face of the deep. In front of her, a tiny table. Miniature meals, a toy bathroom to walk to, even music and a movie—props to invoke the ground. But it never really worked. Airborne, stillborn. A peaceful pause between the nouns and verbs of existence. Ida switched the tape deck at her seat from station to station—modern jazz, Hebrew folk tunes, Italian opera. The sound track for the film, facts about Israel, children's songs in different languages. Her headset was defective; the off switch was broken and the loud-soft dial could not be turned down. She had to take the earphones off entirely or listen at full volume.

The *Bridgeport Post* on microfilm. A June wedding—the bride wore a gown of taffeta, trimmed with pink piping, and carried a bouquet of roses and snapdragons edged with baby's breath. Another picture of Molly and the name of her husband, Nachum Tzvi. Ida gathered loose ends from the last week: the tissue thin ticket to Israel in smudged red ink, Phil's arm outside the blanket, the roll of film in a Connecticut library. Emily Greenspan Tzvi.

Ida could track her through the Jewish Agency in Jerusalem. Perhaps.

Sightseeing. Ida twisted a loop of hair around her thumb. Touring by herself. With no one to cloud the memory of Phil within her or the fetal photographs of the child within Rose or the dreams of the land her father had never seen—Emily's adopted homeland. Emily in faded newsprint, behind a white veil. Not even a glossy picture—just the image beneath the microfiche machine. When Ida tried to touch the face, it dissolved in the shadow of her fingers.

> *Hakshivu, Hakshivu.* Ladies and gentlemen, please give me your attention. If you will look out the windows, those of you on the left side of the aircraft will be able to see *Eretz Yisrael,* the Land of Israel, just coming into view beneath the wing. We welcome you all to the Holy Land! *Haveinu shalom aleichem.* It is our national greeting. May peace be upon you.

A turquoise ribbon of shoreline, a ruffled slip of beach. And then gleaming boxes—buildings like a clutter of frontlets from *tefillin,* only white instead of black. Ida squinted and put her hands on the glass. Years of a concept—words in study and prayer—suddenly congealed into little blocks pushing a blue sea out of her window.

Chagorat Bitachon. The seat belt sign was flashing. In Hebrew, like the words on the exits and menus and airsickness bags. Her father's private world, their special childhood language, was scattered around the plane.

"Excuse me, Miss. Miss? Hello? Could you turn down your . . . . Yes, that's my son's sweater on the floor there. And my newspaper?"

"Here's Dad's paperback, but I can't find the jokers from the cards. Shoshy took them out to play Old Maid. Mom? Mom!"

Ida felt the pressure building in her ears. She put the plastic headphones back on. And swallowed. *Haveinu shalom, shalom, shalom aleichem*. The tune of welcome blasted from her headset.

"Please to keep together as a group, yes? No one should be left behind. Here we have the famous and beautiful Shrine of the Book, erected in 1966 to house the Dead Sea Scrolls found in the caves of Qumran. You know, maybe, of the Essenes, an ascetic sect at the time of Jesus? Notice the white architectural dome in contrast to the black wall behind. This stands for the Sons of Darkness and the Sons of Light. Please to step forward quickly. We go inside now."

The dome loomed behind the tour guide like a porcelain nipple, the clay thrown on a giant potter's wheel. A silhouetted ivory breast. The stone walls surrounding the museum were speckled. Ida walked through the irregular, elliptical arches that framed the openings in a tunnel leading to the inner room where the scroll of Isaiah was wound around a spool encased in plastic. Earlier that morning, Ida had gone to the Jewish Agency. After waiting in lines, filling out forms, and talking with clerks who laughed at her anachronistic phrases, "Sir, if your heart inclineth in my direction, mightn't you assist me in my arduous quest for a long-lost relative?"—the Hebrew her father had taught her was biblical—Ida was finally told to come back tomorrow.

A nun on the tour asked to be shown chapter 53 of Isaiah, the piece of parchment that described the suffering servant. Ida watched the tall woman in her black serge habit and white coif. Just right for Jerusalem in the winter. But in spring or summer, the robe would be unbearable. Ida found the opening section of chapter 40 and read it to the nun. "*Nachamu, nachamu, ami*. Be comforted, my people."

The sister wrote down the words in a composition notebook. Marbled in black and white, and bound so the pages couldn't be torn out; the kind before loose-leaf spiral ones. "The Hebrew itself sounds so soothing. *Nachamu, nachamoo*." She held the final syllable. Back on the bus, Ida sat with the nun.

"We are now approaching *Yad Vashem*, the national memorial to the victims of the Holocaust. The title is also from the book of Isaiah. On this part of our tour you go by yourself. We meet back at the front in an hour, okay? I see you then. You get lost, ask someone for bus 71, and again my name is Ruti."

The nun walked with Ida toward the low museum building. "What does it mean, *Yad Vashem*, do you know?"

Ida tried to think of something in Isaiah that would provide a context. "*Yad* is hand and *shem* means name, but I can't recall the passage that would give it significance." A name and a hand: identity and ability. A sense of self and the grasp of power. Two simple words—perhaps there would be someone she could ask inside.

At the entrance the nun copied the translation beneath a picture of a bearded old man. " 'Remembrance is the root of redemption, forgetfulness the source of exile.' Who was Mr. Tov?"

A face from Hebrew school, in the glossy pages of *Mystics and Masters*. The cover smelled like glue. "A religious leader of the eighteenth century. He founded a movement that dominated Eastern European Jewry up until the time of the Holocaust. They called him the *Baal Shem Tov*, the owner of the good name."

Together they began their descent into the lower rooms of the museum. Mounted on the walls were anti-Semitic slogans, newspaper stories about the rise of Nazism, German edicts requiring yellow stars. And then photographs—piles of skeletal corpses, gas chambers, ovens. Enlarged newsprint, with the black dots showing. In one picture a father clutched his daughter while an SS officer with a rifle fired at them from a few feet away. The little girl was wearing a winter coat. "Over a million children."

Members of the tour group waited in an antechamber near the exit. Ida and the nun sat down on a bench next to a red haired woman who was wiping her face with a wash-and-dry.

"It's the woolen coat." Ida held down her eyelids with her fingers. "That coat with the felt collar. I've seen so many little girls in winter coats like that."

With her head bowed, the nun was lost in her voluminous cloth. So much material—enough for a tablecloth or bedspread or drapes. "What act of goodness can ever offset this outrage, this violation?"

The red-haired woman handed her pocketbook to a man who was rolling up the visitors' guide. She took off her glasses and rubbed them on her skirt. "Hal and I came here a number of years ago. This is our second time. Seeing this—of course we knew about it before, but actually looking into the faces of those people, starved and tortured, just killed like flies—well, seeing these pictures the first time, we decided to have another child. Our third. I was in my thirties then."

Hal's camera case dangled beneath his armpit from the thin strap that crossed his chest. Other black attachments were clipped to his belt. "One visit was enough. It's so terrible to . . . We probably shouldn't have come here again, but it was on the tour. I'm sorry we came. You forget, you know, and . . . I think we shouldn't have come back."

"We're not very religious, mind you. In fact, we're pretty much assimilated. But in the face of this, being Jewish, it means something different." The couple showed Ida and the nun some snapshots of their children. Off-center, holding a hose and tomato plants, cut off at the waist by the bottom of the picture. "That was taken when we put in the new patio."

"Where are you from?" Ida moved the photo to the back of the stack and looked at a springer spaniel cornered in a breezeway.

"Portland, Oregon." She pointed to their daughter in the next shot, balancing a briefcase in front of her knees. "Hal's in the insurance business."

"I teach college." Ida flipped to a photo of balloons and birthday cake.

"Oh, how nice. What subjects? This year I took a night course at our community college. In Psych, called *Adjustment*. Good lectures, but too much reading for me."

On the bus, they talked about adult education and nondegree programs. Not the child in the winter coat.

9

The sun was beginning to set. Ida followed the narrow streets, flanked by houses and enclosed courtyards, down to the *Kotel,* the one remaining wall from Herod's reconstruction of Solomon's Temple in the heart of David's city. The archways yawned at the cobbled paving; the smell of soup leaked from upper windows. A Moslem call to prayer slid between two notes. Tentatively, from far off, like an afterthought. Ida stopped to loosen the inner strap of her sandal. Yesterday she had spent three hours at the Jewish Agency before a full day of touring—only on her third visit this morning had someone been able to locate the name of Emily's kibbutz. Did her mother and Nachum still live there? No one knew. The main switchboard at *Kfar Blum* had been out of order, and when Ida finally reached the office, a volunteer answered the phone who was unfamiliar with the name Tzvi and couldn't find a members' list. Just two more days. On Thursday, her flight would leave from Tel Aviv; by evening she'd be back in Boston. Should she actually look for Emily? Perhaps the names were enough, and any information they might bring her. Or maybe she would go and see Emily but pretend to be someone else—a research assistant studying collective farms? The president of a charitable American foundation? A daughter of distant relatives?

Ida did not take the direct route to the Western Wall

but wandered through the Armenian section and the ancient Jewish Quarter. In one paved square, between a dry goods store and a construction dump, she found a twisted tree stump protected by a low abutment. A branch with healthy foliage had been grafted to the old trunk. Ida smiled at the hybrid marriage. "Ah, these dry bones."

Burnt umber—the color between copper and yellow in paint sets. Ida's olive skirt began to blend with the rough-cut Jerusalem stone, which glowed with the sun's memory. Only a few lights twinkled on the hillside. Like grounded stars. Ida approached the steps and landings leading down to the Wailing Wall. She sat on the parapet lining the walkway.

In the courtyard below, people clustered at the far end near the *Kotel*. A blank retaining wall—for two thousand years her people's most sacred site. The upper part was cluttered with smaller bricks while the heavy, ponderous rocks lay farther down. No two blocks were identical, and tufts of green grew in the crevices.

The Wall. On posters and postcards, printed on hotel stationery, etched in patina. Even stamped on cocktail napkins under hot tea served in glasses. Ida remembered the judge's chambers with the glare between the venetian blinds. "No, Your Honor, the past should not be buried, particularly when it's painful." She spoke aloud, "We are the people who dig up old stones and still curse the wrongs of Amalek."

Ida did not go down to the Wall as the worshipers below brought on the evening twilight. *Barchu*—we bless You, Lord who is blessed. Ida caught the opening line of the service and hummed the first word to herself. It stretched across four notes, an ascending scale in a major key. With no half tones. She did not notice the shadow of a figure sitting behind her on the landing.

"It is a moving sight, no?"

She turned quickly. A white shirt above baggy, khaki pants. Dark eyes under bangs. "Why are you watching me?" Ida reached for the handbag she had put down.

"Because I am one of the few living Israelis who likes tourists. How do you do." He bowed—a hand in the front, the other in back. "My name is Menachem Baruch."

Unlike the muscular, suntanned soldiers who made the inside of Israeli buses competing tourist attractions, this fellow looked like a remnant from prewar Poland. Except that his shirt was unbuttoned halfway to his waist. He spoke English with only the trace of an accent.

Menachem walked up to Ida and stood too close. "What I like about tourists is that they see everything fresh. No reruns. Tell me, what have you been looking at so intently?"

"How long have you been following me?" From the jumbled prayers below, an echoed melody: *l'olam vaed.*

"Oh, a while. I hope you do not mind. I didn't want to disturb you." With one hand he caressed the other in a slow, delicate gesture. "You said something about Amalek?"

"Where did you learn your English?"

"In New York. I am a filmmaker, and the opportunities in Israel are somewhat limited." Op-pore-tee-unities, the syllables ringing like a china bell. He lifted a piece of lint from Ida's blouse and held it up with exaggerated precision. "Come, we go down to the Wall."

Ida took a sweater out of her tote bag and wrapped it around her shoulders. Menachem extended his hand, bent back at the wrist, his elbow cocked in a sharp V. Ida thought of the illustrations from the Golden Books for children. *The Prince and the Pauper, The Story of King Midas*, where the lords and attendants had elongated limbs. Always in awkward positions. On the hand she declined to hold, Menachem wore a modern watch whose face had no numbers.

"A warm day for December. Very unusual." He swayed from side to side as he walked.

"Yes."

"So, won't you please, tell me what you see in our Wall?"

Ida looked ahead at the *Kotel*, growing browner, grainier as the sky darkened. "I see the recognition of an end—this far, and no further."

"Ah, you need ends to have beginnings. Yes, I like that."

She put her arms into the knit sleeves. "A wall says stop. It says no. This week I visited *Yad Vashem*. No. Never again."

Guards inspected Ida's purse and frisked Menachem perfunctorily at the edge of the open expanse leading to the Wall. Menachem covered his head with one hand while searching in his pocket. "I thought I had a handkerchief . . ." He finally borrowed some tissue from Ida. Then he blew his nose in it. "But tell me what the Wall means to *you*. I am a collector. I save stories. One of my hobbies is to come here when I'm bored, to gather anecdotes from around the world, stories about the Wall."

A peculiar man. Ida watched him roll up the Kleenex and stuff it in his pocket. A merchant of tales. An Israeli who bowed. He kept up his pants with a wide belt that had a shiny buckle, but his worn-out loafers were cracked. "Well, Menachem, I'll tell you. Why not? I was not looking at the Wall that is left but at the piece that is missing. It's like half a horse in a painting by Van Dyck; you can't think of half a horse. The part shown on the canvas naturally recalls the part left out."

"Um, you are a smart lady." He was not looking at her face.

"Unlike most *ladies* who are dumb, you mean."

"Now, I did not say that." They walked closer to the Wall where spotlights turned the courtyard into a wide stage that was hard underfoot. Ida felt uncomfortable. Like at job interviews.

"Then you have come to the Wall to look for missing pieces, have you? What pieces are you lacking?"

She thought of broken rocks. The oldest and the newest, the stones from her past and those to toss into the future. Those washed up on the shore, and the flat ones that skip across the surface of waves when you throw them sideways. "*Eylu va eylu,*" she translated into Hebrew. "I'm a teacher, Menachem. Sometimes my students write long papers because they don't have time to write short ones. Me too. I'm too tired tonight not to talk. Especially here, with all this history . . ." Ida told Menachem about her desire for a child, which had led to her mother at *Kfar Blum*. The evening grew darker; the stars in the sky winked at those on the ground. The Wall glowed in the floodlights. Burnt umber.

Menachem waited for her to look back at him. "I don't have a car, but I can borrow one. If you like, I will drive you tomorrow to *Kfar Blum*."

"Why?" She didn't want to feel obligated. Or lead him on. A sweet fellow, as harmless as he was unattractive. He had rolled down one sleeve, which was missing the cuff button.

"No, I spoke too soon. We should go for a cup of coffee, talk some more, then I offer, yes?"

"That's very kind of you, thank you, but . . ."

"Listen to them praying over there. 'In forever love the House of Israel loves You.' Loved with love, blessed with blessing. In English it always comes out redundant. I think in the Eden Garden the peach trees peached peaches."

"Garden of Eden. Menachem, you are very generous to . . ."

"Please, hear me. You do not want a boyfriend, I see that. This is not, how you call it?—a pass. Just, simply, a help. American Jews give money, yes? Not to buy anything from us, just to connect. We need to connect also. What I give, sometimes, is directions. Usually I walk the people where they're going. You gave me a story—let me give you a ride."

"But I haven't even decided yet whether or not to go."

His brow rippled like cloth gathered on a taut thread. Then the string broke. "Haven't you, my dear? Then what are you doing here in Israel, halfway round the world, talking to a wall?"

Ida slipped into a seat at the rear of the classroom and edged her chair closer to the corner. The cinder block was overpainted, leaving hardened dry dribbles below all the windows. A pleasant, sparse room. Ida put the black looseleaf in her lap and strained for a normal, businesslike smile. The woman up front turned from the waist, nodded politely, and resumed her stance, arms raised, back to Ida. Ida's heart was beating in her upper lip. Even from behind: the only blood relative she had ever seen. In person.

The students, standing in rows, ignored the silent observer; in a skirt suit, surely an American. All eyes were on the music teacher. Ida automatically translated the Hebrew to herself, the English instant-replay echoing behind the crisp, direct language.

"*Ode pa'am*. Once again now. Without mistakes. Watch the ending. Ilana, breathe deeply—a fuller sound on the solo. One, two, three, and . . ."

The room resounded with singing, a panoply of interwoven melody. Not harmony, but a counterpoint of two tunes as a third trilled along in a higher key. "*L'boker ha'adom*, to a red morning, the little bird replied we must sing *shalom*."

The room was large. The class was less than half over. The teacher would certainly not turn around. Ida had plenty of time; she could compose herself later, and even if anyone noticed, so what?—a sappy American. The tears welled up in her eyes as the arms up front danced to her mother's music—arms with strong hands and thin wrists like Ida's.

"*Tov me'od.* Very good. Very good. Oh, we've run late. Go quickly now. A good start on the new numbers. Shira, remember to work on those voice exercises in the lower register, and everyone: LEARN THE WORDS. Yes. Thanks, Margolit. The piano part sounded much better today. Until tomorrow." Said in the back of her mouth, not up close to the teeth—the residue of an American accent.

Ida stood up in the empty room. The conductor walked toward her. "*Shalom*. Welcome. I'm Malka. Chaim told me just before class that you'd be sitting in. Are you doing some sort of music study?"

Ida's hand trembled in Malka's. "Not exactly. I'm interviewing immigrants from the States who came to Israel and settled on kibbutzim. They told me you might be free around lunch. I have a modest grant, I can't really offer you anything for your time, but I do make it a policy to meet over a nice dinner. If there's a restaurant that's not too far away—it would give us some privacy, so we wouldn't be disturbed." With the cadence of a nervous graduate student.

"I have a better idea. I know a lovely spot in the hills. I like to go there and unwind after a hectic morning. I've been up since five. No one will bother us there, and we can bring bag lunches from the dining hall. Better than wasting time in a car. How's that sound? And anyway, such warm, unseasonable weather. It's quite unusual this time of year."

Ida followed her mother out of the classroom. "The

music was just beautiful. I particularly liked the last piece. I never heard it before."

"Oh, thank you. It's mine. I write children's songs. The music classes here give me a built-in incentive, with people to hear and perform my scores. It's terrible to write for strangers—phantoms out there, you know? But these kids are real, and very special. I love them all."

At the kitchen behind the dining area Malka ordered the food in a sharp voice she hadn't used with her pupils. Ida noticed the gray strands in her curly, dark hair. Her features were well defined.

Climbing along a rocky path. Ida lost her footing in low-heeled shoes. "Tell me, Emily, were you already married when you came here?" One of the few answers Ida already knew.

A slower walking pace. "How did you know my name was Emily?"

"Well, uh, let me see. I always make a point of keeping careful records, and I don't have those notes with me at the moment, but . . . No, I remember now, the Jewish Agency had you listed that way in their files, and I figured Malka was the Hebrew root of Molly." Not quite convincing. Oh please, not yet. Not until the top of the hill.

"So, they listed my nickname too?" Mother and daughter walked on in silence.

They reached Molly's spot. A guarded thicket, tall trees framing a view of the Golan Heights. "Here, we can eat on this rock in the shade." The air clear and warm, bright sun, and pebbly dirt dry as dust.

Malka unwrapped her sandwich. Ida stood still. Then

sat, took off her shoes; she dramatized relief. Picked up the brown lunch bag, put it down. "Molly, I'm not really working on a grant. Research of another sort, I guess. But I wanted to talk to you alone. I couldn't think of a better way. I hope you'll forgive me."

The older woman nodded. "Who are you?"

"Please understand, Molly—Malka. I don't want to intrude into your life. I can be gone again as though I never came, like a dream. No one ever has to know. But if I were you—and I have no right to assume you're like me—I know that. But I would want to know, just once, so many years later, when it no longer hurt, what happened to her. And for me, I had to find out for *my* child if it mattered, if knowing mattered. Or maybe it already mattered more than I knew."

Malka's expression clouded. Ida hurried, bearing down to land her thoughts. "I was born on October twelfth, thirty-nine years ago, as Ida Greenspan." Her head pounding. Looking down.

Malka, with egg and tomato still in her mouth. So softly, "*Baruch Hashem.*" Blessed be the Name.

10

"How did you find me?"

"The original birth certificate at the Department of Health, then the high school yearbook in the Bridgeport Library, then the wedding announcement in the newspaper, finally the Jewish Agency."

"That's all?"

"No, not really. I guess I'd been learning to search, that *I* should, for a long time. When I studied, when I learned languages. I taught my students to ask, even the harder questions without answers."

"And your parents?"

"The very best. Loving, giving. Limited, in some respects, but solid, caring. Even when we were most divergent."

"Then you didn't tell them?"

"Her. My father, may he rest in peace, died many years ago. But my mother, I think she'd be upset by all this—unfinished business. She's more comfortable with product than process. All my moves have been hard on her—different cities and homes and jobs, the same for all my friends, really, not rooted in the earth any more. She thinks I'm, well, flighty." Ida thought of Mildred, trimming the lilacs every year in front of the house. Snipping with the long shears. In gardening gloves. "Not that birds are better than trees, you understand, but it's wrong to ground one or uproot the other. Anyway, *I* needed to know, not her."

"But your mother did move when *she* had to, didn't she? After all, she went in search of you. When the apples didn't drop right off the tree, so to speak. She couldn't have a child of her own, I presume."

"Not till later on, after my adoption, when she gave birth to my sister. But yes, you're right. I suppose she did move."

And through the afternoon. The sky streaked with red. "Where were my grandparents from? Do you have any pictures of them? My father's name? What was he like? Why didn't you marry each other? Do I have half sisters, and brothers? What type of child were you? What traits run in our family? Did you want to give me up?"

Talking down the path. Borrowing Menachem's car to drive to a restaurant for dinner.

"I was young, Ida. I loved him, or thought I did. We wanted to marry, but his father felt my family unsuitable. Poor Russian stock, *prust*, common. And we were so young. And then there was the issue of college for him. He couldn't buck his father, in the end." They walked together outside, away from the waitresses and customers.

"Ida, I was terrified. So alone and abandoned, with you growing inside, secretly, the source of my shame and terror. Nowhere to kindle a flicker of joy. How could I? Where was the love I thought he felt, that I felt? And now the fruit of affection was taking over my life, trapping me. Like a cancer." They held hands.

"But still, I do remember, quiet moments when the boat stopped pitching. I was sick all the time. But late at night, alone in my room, feeling you kick within me. The wonder of it. And I did want you." They couldn't find a bench to sit on and returned to the car. Ida let the motor run for the heater. Then turned it off, parked by the side of the road. The car cooled slowly.

"What I would have wanted most? To travel with my parents to some Caribbean island, to have the baby far away and return with it, with him—I did want a boy, not another girl to suffer. A little man to replace Will. Someone to avenge me someday against Mr. Lessing? Who knows. How I hated that man! And the power he wielded over his son, and so over me. I was very young, Ida. Well, if my parents could just have pretended that the baby was my new little brother, like in some movie I once saw. And then, too, someone to carry on the name Greenspan. My father had always wanted a boy, and I was an only child."

"And then I was born a girl."

"Yes, that too. Nor had we any money for Caribbean islands. And could we really live a lie? Would that have been best for you, after all? Would Will and the Lessings never tell? We'd be at their mercy. And would I lie to you too? And, then, would I ever find a husband that way?"

"In retrospect, Malka?"

"In retrospect, if only I could have known about Nachum! Strong, loving Nachum. He would have wanted me anyhow, *and* the baby, you. But would I ever have met him if I kept you? Could I have convinced my parents to let me go to Israel for a year along with a baby? As it was, they only agreed to let me go after I'd suffered months and months of such depression that they were willing to try anything. Before that, they had found me a job as a receptionist in a dental office. All day long, with that drill in the background. Drilling and drilling. After work, I'd come home, go upstairs and read, and sleep. I never wanted to leave my room. I was very young, Ida. I don't know exactly when I started fighting back, trying to leave the country. I had to go away to start to heal."

The clock above the portable refrigerator read 11:15 by the time Malka returned. She stared at the yellow and black upholstery fading on the furniture. Imitation Danish. The couch looked just the way it did after a weekend in Tel Aviv or a nature hike in the Negev. Always the same when she came home, but a different size.

"Oh, Nachum! Where is Nachum?" Malka wandered toward the food cabinet wedged between the sink and the wall. Opened it. After all these years. With my eyes, and I remember Will in the shape of her mouth.

Below. A bottle of wine she'd been saving. A present. Looking for the corkscrew.

On the table, a note from Nachum: "Where have you been? Stopping over Chaim's, 10:15."

Put back the wine. A little Sabra would be better. Swishing around in the bottom of a large glass. Cut crystal, from her mother. Strangely out of place here.

Sabra glowing in the back of her throat, and chocolate oranges when she breathed out. Then the screen door bouncing closed.

"Malka, I was beginning to wonder. I got your message that you wouldn't be back until after dinner. Where were you? Malka?"

"Not here, Nachum." A college professor. And a writer like me. "Oh Nachum."

On his way to the stove to boil water, he noticed the liquor. "My God, Malka, what is it? What's happened?"

The miniature jade plant growing in a teapot was a green blur; Malka focused her eyes near it but not on it.

"A woman came to my class today to observe. Said at first she was doing a study. Nachum, it was—my daughter." Looking into his face, "No, of course not. Hadassah is at Columbia. We spoke to her only yesterday on the phone! This child—I once—you remember . . ."

They sat together on the couch, Nachum in the middle, knees apart, elbows on his thighs, supporting a wine glass by the bulb as if it had no stem. Malka faced him at an angle, her bare feet under her, hugging her knees. All night long, putting words on it. Shock, elation, dislocation, regret, continuity, estrangement, affinity.

"Remember Lot's wife? I had to leave without a glance behind." Will Lessing, with soft brown hair on his upper lip, which she could only see when close enough to kiss. To other people it was invisible, hiding there quietly, waiting to grow. "I wish I could talk to him too, once more." Sniffling, the last time, at the end of the black curly cord from the hall phone, snaking down the wall to where she sat on the floor. Will? Will? I can't hear you. His father roaring in the background. That boy and his two-bit whore! Accept her? Support them? I'll be damned if I will!

"It was Ida, you know, who convinced me to marry you." He slanted the glass, but the liquor stayed level.

"Nachum Tzvi! What are you talking about?"

"I remember the night you told me about her, after the dig at Tel Hazor. We'd had that trouble with the water, remember? In the evening, overlooking the Huleh . . . the way you talked about it, what had happened, your family—that's when I first decided to marry you."

"I couldn't believe, then, that it didn't make a difference to you."

"Of course it did, Malka. It made a difference that you told me."

She'd cut herself at the start of the dig. A clean slice between the thumb and index finger. "They'd given me something for the infection and the pain. All that night, I remember my hand was numb." Malka traced one finger across the fine-lined C of a scar that reached to the knuckle. "Maybe I wouldn't have told you without the codeine."

"That Bunya, the nurse. Remember her? She never knew what she was doing! You're lucky they didn't amputate."

Nachum had moved to the corner of the couch after Malka made some coffee. Finishing it, he draped his arms around her from behind, the empty cup still in his hand.

"She's a little like Lev, Nachum. Just a little." That inflection in her voice at the end of a phrase, taking a quick breath in the middle of a sentence. "How can that be, Nachum? Something like speech patterns, could they be hereditary? And in another language, yet!" His arms hung like a lei around her neck; she traced circles in the hair. "Forty years, almost. Imagine, Nachum. Nearly forty years since I saw her last."

"Forty years. That's how long it takes to get out of Bridgeport and send your daughter to graduate school."

"And in between—my mother was making a wedding at Aunt Celia's rented beach house, and Hadassah was born six weeks premature, and the kibbutz added on the new school wing . . ."

"And the year in New York after your father got sick, and coming back for the war before Lev was born."

"And the first song I had recorded."

"And the three thousandth time we made love," caressing the side of her breast. An old joke.

Malka gave him her lips. "So who's counting?"

The light was beginning to come through the wooden slats that shaded the window. "You still up, Nach?"

"Um."

"She's thinking of having a baby."

"Um."

"You know what that makes me? Nachum, you're asleep, aren't you?"

"No, Bubbe Tzvi, I'm awake." He flung one arm over her buttocks for proof.

"And she's not married any more. I wonder what her mother will say."

Ida leaned against the window of dancing stars as the car jostled over the road back to Jerusalem. Menachem drove the way he walked, weaving from side to side, speeding up and slowing down. Meandering. Me and. Bump. Er ing. Bump. She knew she should talk to him—after he'd brought her to the kibbutz and waited around the whole afternoon and half the night. But to wrap it up, to paper it in concepts and a ribbon of words, to hear the loss in translation . . .

"It's okay, Ida, you don't have to talk. Silence is nice, too. Maybe later, say, in an hour. The rule is, no speaking until after midnight. Starting now."

Me and. Bump. Me and. Bump. The car door jiggled like a crib rocked by the bars. Outside, the sky reached down to the ground, snug behind the edges of the black trees. That same dark hug from her first overnight, the children singing campfire songs and "I Believe." Her father's moonlight beckoning to the beach from its sparkling watery runway. Oh holy night, crouching off the Maine coast, where she and Phil had lured it toward the rocks.

"For He is my rock and my salvation." The funereal refrain, ". . . bound up in the bond of everlasting life." Flesh of my flesh. No longer an island, cut off from the mainland: Ida remembered Malka's hand in hers, the same fleshy palms and short fingers.

Potholes. Ida was thrown against the armrest as the car turned a corner. Menachem pointed to the seat belt. "And maybe to put it on, to be safe."

Don't start a sentence with a conjunction. She'd written

it on hundreds of papers. Fumbling for the buckle, "Sh, you're breaking the rules." Syntax and context, and now a beginning: Malka's face and story filled the blank page.

If only she could tell Phil! But what? Yes, ma'am, we have reached your party. Go ahead. You have three minutes before you'll be disconnected. Three minutes. Phil? Her wrists are like mine and we hugged. Lilting tunes, songs about birds, and a frightened boyfriend with my eyes.

Ida spoke first. "Do you know, Menachem, I'm a *Kohen*! I always wondered when they called people up to the Torah in synagogue. And suddenly, after all this time—an Israelite by default—I find I'm a descendant of the priestly tribe."

"*You*, a woman, say blessings?"

"Certainly. At the university, I attend services where everyone participates equally."

His ears moved when he smiled. "I myself hardly ever go to *shul*. I guess I serve the Lord by chauffeuring his lost lady priests!"

Me and. Bump. Me and. Ring. If only Phil were here. To dance with, to talk all night. Ida had tried not to think of him, arching above her. Or sitting on top of the radiator guard. Or combing the locks that hung down to cover where sideburns didn't grow. After shaving for her. Or shaving for Marge? In Palo Alto. Ida looked at Menachem slouched behind the wheel.

"Ida, I make a suggestion to you, yes? And you can say no if you are uncomfortable. How about we stop in Deganya, a couple of hours from Jerusalem. They have a restaurant and guest house. Tomorrow we could leave early. Be back in Jerusalem by eight, even, if you like. And maybe now you're getting hungry." She didn't respond right away. "Sometimes it's good just to stop moving, no?"

"Yes. Okay, Menachem, if you're sure we won't get a late start."

But the restaurant was already closed. Ida stayed in the car as Menachem arranged for the rooms. With the headlights off, darkness seeped into the car. She uncrossed her feet, plunging her legs in. Knee-deep in the black emptiness. Her lap glowed green from the tiny bulb above the dashboard—Menachem's door was open a crack since the safety belt had fallen outside on the gravel.

Menachem came out of the building and stood for a moment on the porch. He scuffed his feet and stared over his stomach at his shoes, then lit a match for a cigarette, changed his mind, and threw away the light. He walked the long way around the back of the car. The seat groaned as he eased himself halfway in.

"What's the matter, no room at the inn?"

He kept his eyes on the steering wheel, sheathed in perforated leather. "Yes, they have a room. *A* room." Picking at the sides where the leather had worn away, "I drive on if you like? Or, you know I think by now, I am a gentleman. Not to bother you, and I sleep on the floor." With the motor off the car was growing chilly.

Ida shook her head slowly. Between exhaustion and amusement: "Oh, shit."

"I drive." He started the car.

"No, don't." She put her hand on his arm. "You're too tired, and so am I. I trust you. Come on. We'll take the room."

Menachem bounded out of the car. "And never mind about the restaurant. Look, I bring a peekneek." Out of the dented trunk he lifted a plastic milk crate, "liberated from Super-Sol," stuffed with mesh bags and a rumpled sheet.

Inside, Menachem pushed the twin beds together and spread the sheet over both. Then he unpacked a bottle of wine, some cheese and bread, two apples, and a canister of *tahina*. "Even napkins, see? Very fancy, everything but ants."

She looked in the bathroom for some glasses, but there were none. "No matter, we can drink from the bottle." They used the napkins in place of plates. Menachem cut the bread with his pocket knife and then chipped away at the cork in the bottle.

"So, your mother, did you like her?" Pieces of cork were dropping on the sheet.

"Yes. Oh, yes." Ida began to peel the wax off the cheese. It came apart perfectly in two hollow moons, red reminders of the flattened yellow globe.

"And brothers and sisters you have? Half sisters, that is?"

She smiled slowly. "Yes. Both."

"I think you are now an honorary Israeli, no? A step-Sabra, how you call it—once removed?" They laughed.

"I never did know what that meant. Speaking of removal, just push the cork in. Who cares. I also never understood what the big deal was about not getting the cork in the wine."

He offered her the bottle. Israeli white wine. She drank long, and then he took it for himself. "This is a kiss once removed." He put his lips where hers had been. "It is sad, too? You wish she had kept you? Then you grow up with real mother in your real country."

"Oh no, Menachem. My mother in America is my *real* mother. This one is my past, my history."

"Prehistoric, maybe. Like this country to you. I am right?"

"Not that remote. Like distant family and relatives. My immediate family is in the States."

"I hear sometimes that secondhand children—"

"Adopted."

"Yes, adopted. That adopted children feel, uh, not just right. Not, well, the same."

"More so, usually. Not less. You know, there are no 'accidents' in adoption, no kids born because after midnight the drugstore closed, or because the diaphragm didn't fit, or the in-laws were pressuring. With adoption, there's plenty of time to back out. Adoptive parents, on the whole, are probably a little better than the natural kind."

They passed the bottle again. "I was thinking," Menachem stared at his hands, his fingernails thick and blunt. "You said you look for your mother to help you decide does your child need a father to find. But you don't talk about that father, just your mother. Maybe I ask too personal. You tell me. But you will look for him, or no?"

She would. Malka had given Ida his name and that of his parents. But Menachem was right. It was her mother she really sought. Ida felt dizzy. A fine, floating feeling. "I'd better have some cheese with that wine."

"According to our law, a Jew is the child of a Jewish mother. The father doesn't count." Menachem propped some pillows against the wall at the head of the bed. "Come, you sit up here. Okay?"

"Okay." Ida crawled over beside him and dipped a piece of cheese in the *tahina*. "Here."

"No, dip the bread. You're not supposed to put in the cheese."

"Why not?" She tasted it. "It's good. It's very good."

Menachem moved his pillow aside and edged down until he lay flat on the bed, munching his apple, with knees up and one hand behind his head. "My back is not good. Ah, straight feels better when the spine is weak." Ida sat cross-legged, cutting her apple into slices. "Ida, your Catholic friend—"

"Rose."

"What you told me at the Wall. I have been thinking of it very much. How did she feel about, well, it is not so, I don't know the word in English, not clean, uh, without passion of course, that way to be pregnant?"

"Antiseptic. I've thought of it too. Rose said it was like a doctor's examination. Neutral. Mildly unpleasant, maybe. She had to remind herself that something important was happening."

Menachem was easy to talk to, a man Ida would probably never see again. Her words sounded distant, with no echo.

"Ida, you will do that? Like going to the dentist? Or maybe, you have a friend who cares for you some?"

She lay down too. "Yes, I love someone who loves me as well."

"He does not want to marry you?"

"I don't know, but it doesn't matter. He's already married."

"But you would marry *him*?"

The ceiling was patched with acoustic tiles. Ida resisted the temptation to count them. "He isn't Jewish. Anyway, it's not a question I'll ever have to face."

"And he wouldn't, out of love for you—"

"It's more complicated. Would he want to be with me when the child was born? Would we put his name on the birth certificate? Would he assume any financial responsibility or visit the child later, and who would we say he was?" And what would he say to his wife? "The other way is simple. But sterile."

Menachem turned onto his side. Then he sat up. "And when must *you* decide?"

"I don't know. Soon."

"Ida, I know I am not so much to look at. And you are such a beautiful woman. I, if I could help—" He curled his lip over his upper teeth. "I would be honored."

The conditioned reflex—say no; yes can always come later. "Oh Menachem." She kissed him softly. "Surely *I* would be honored, were I ready to make that decision."

Finally he slept. She relaxed. Why not? The irritating question, like sand in the bed. The light from the bathroom lit his face, poorly shaven. His mouth slightly open. Hair sprouted down his neck. So why not? Ida looked at his eyelids, smooth and pink like baby birds before the feathers grew. Would she say no if his back were muscular, his hands large? If he looked like Phil? If it weren't for Phil? She thought of Phil kissing her, his eyes open. The way he licked against her mouth playfully, like a puppy, or sometimes quickly, like a snake, before sinking in deeper. Menachem flinched and then lay still again. His eyebrows moved on the bridge of his nose.

Why not? Why must crooked teeth eclipse a gentle soul? Flesh, Ida thought, that wouldn't melt. Even for a teacher of literature, a lover of ideas. She rolled over onto her stomach.

Rose always said they were superficial, that type. Men chasing after bodies. Predators, she called them, "carnal consumers." Who couldn't see Rose beneath her robe of fat. But Ida was supposed to know better. Had she joined the enemy camp? Aesthetics or just instinct? She burrowed under the covers, squirming toward the edge of the bed, away from Menachem.

Why not? The shadow of her own head against the wall blended with images of crowning infants and Malka's dark hair. Longer hair than in the high school yearbook. The blanket on the bed smelled like mothballs.

11

"Yes, sir. I'm checking. The flight into New York was on time. Your party should be on the ten o'clock shuttle into Boston."

10:25. Good. She'll be here within twenty minutes. With too many bags. Sunburned, maybe? Is it summer now in Israel?

It was summer in Palo Alto. Almost. Marge had been sunburned, a little. Her hair the color of taffy, she had smelled like sea shells. And freckles. He'd forgotten about freckles. She was so tall. No need to stay on his elbows. He'd gotten used to staying on his elbows, and to curly hair.

If I walk quickly, I can probably get through security and down to the gate. No briefcase for the metal detector. Chances are they won't ask to see a ticket.

10:35. It takes a little longer, even when the plane's on time. Taxiing over to the jetway and all. But still, fifteen minutes at most, her lips between mine. And her dark hair falling out of the clip in the back.

Marge had let her hair grow. It parted behind like a curtain for her neck. And in the palm of his hand, a bunch of glossy fingernails. He hadn't remembered fingernails.

She'll probably be tired. A thirteen-hour flight. But she might have slept on the plane. Rose will be at work. Or maybe we can stop back at my place. To pick up the mail. Maybe we won't make it to her house.

He thought of Ida, so tight around him. So tight it was hard to wait, to be good to her at first. Marge had felt loose and wet, like entering the ocean. Her legs up around him. Easy to be the perfect lover, to time himself. He wished he could last that long for Ida.

Here they come. Well, she wouldn't be the first off. Have to collect her stuff and get down her coat, with someone helping her, being so short. Maybe she sat near the back. Kept walking until she got a window. My luck, she'll be the very last. Using the rest room after they landed.

Surely there are more passengers. Getting a few extra carry-ons stored at the rear. Why would the stewardess leave before the last passenger?

"I'm sorry, sir, there's definitely no one else on board. Maybe your friend took another airline."

But she said the shuttle. And El Al was on time into New York. If anything changed, she was to call from Kennedy or LaGuardia. I didn't leave until after ten, in case she needed to reach me.

Wait here another hour for the next shuttle? But what if she's trying to phone me at home? Or at the office. I could call her house—no, Rose would be at work so there'd be no one to answer.

Maybe something happened. What if she got sick in Israel? Or had an accident? What if she found her mother and decided to stay longer. And miss the start of classes? She couldn't call me in California. I never called Rose.

"Phil Manning, wouldn't you know it! You just getting in from the West Coast?"

"Oh, Tom. Uh, no. I got in late yesterday. Switched my

flight, actually. Stayed a few days longer than I'd planned to."

"What a surprise seeing you here. I just arrived from Philly. Debby and the kids are staying till Sunday with her mother, but I escaped. So, what are you doing here? Phil? Hey Phil, are you with me?"

"Oh, sorry. I was supposed to meet someone, but it seems they're not on the plane."

"A female someone, huh? Don't tell me the great Phil Manning, single married wonder of the Western Hemisphere, has been stood up! Anybody I know?"

"Knock it off, Tom. No, you don't know her." Maybe I should call her mother in Connecticut. But if nothing's wrong, that would alarm her. And who am I to Mrs. Morgan?

"Buddy, do you think you could give me a ride to the office? I left my car there last week."

I could try to reach Rose at the hospital. I wonder if she has an office or works on rounds.

"Phil? What do you say? It's not much out of your way if you're heading home. Where are you going now?"

"I don't know, Tom. I'm trying to figure that out. Okay. Sure. But let's get your luggage and hurry, all right?"

"Sure. Thanks. If something's fouled up, I'm sure she'll try to reach you at the office or home. Where else?"

Phil switched into the left-hand lane. Waited at the light. "You got some change for the toll? The exact change booth will be faster." Damn! Why the hell is the traffic tied up *now*? It isn't rush hour. "What is this?"

"Phil, relax. There must be an accident up ahead. Calm

down. There's nothing you can do about it anyway. Come, let's talk. Take your mind off it. How's Marge these days?"

An accident up ahead. He shifted into neutral and raced the motor. "Fine, Tom, she's just fine."

"Hm. Do I detect a sour note there? Trouble in paradise?"

"Paradise? Crap. You think it's paradise to have a wife who lives three thousand miles away making twice your salary and no kids?"

"After two weeks with Debby's mother and Andrew biting Amy, it sounds like heaven to me. Not to mention Ms. Mystery lost on a plane."

"Christ, Tom, between you and Mast I've had about as much jealousy as I can stomach. You want to get laid, why don't you just go do it and stop projecting all your henpecked fantasies on me." Phil turned off the car. "What the hell is going on in that goddamn tunnel!"

"Hey, calm down. And have a little pity for Mast. Twenty-five years with Kay and it's a wonder he can remember what there is to be jealous about. Listen, you don't have to be so sensitive. Mast looks at you and sees a man with freedom and a dynamic woman like Marge—it's a compliment, you asshole—a wife who encourages you to see other women; I bet you two *discuss* it! And she comes up to visit now and then, and you fly off on romantic little vacations that she sponsors, plus God knows what else you've got on the side. How do you think we're going to feel when we can't afford even the day camp any more, and all Debby can talk about is her new exercise class!"

"Debby's every bit as intelligent as Marge, for God's sake. What's the matter, you two have a fight?"

"You're damn right she is, and that's why when we look at Marge we think—there, that's what Debby and Kay could have been if they'd taken jobs instead of raising kids and putting us through graduate school. And straightening the house all the time in place of the cleaning lady I can't afford. So you think it's hell when you miss a connection with some broad? If you get bored, you can stop by and walk the dog at my house so she won't shit on the rug like the last time I had two days alone three years ago. That was during the ice storm."

Maybe she was bumped off the flight in Israel. She could have had trouble getting a line to the States. I'll check at home for a cable. "Finally, the traffic's easing up. Tom, let's drop it. Thanks to your mother-in-law and Eastern Airlines, we're yelling over nothing."

"Yah, you're right. Hey, you know what Ricky told his grandmother yesterday? We were all sitting at the dinner table . . ."

I'll drive over to her place and leave a note. That'll cover things in case somehow she gets in late. Maybe they lost her luggage in New York. But she would have called.

"Did you hear that? Right in front of the old biddy."

"Listen, I'll just drop you off out front. Tom, look, just forget it if I'm out of sorts, okay?"

"Sure. Vacations are the pits. When you stop running, you see the cracks in the sidewalk instead of a blur."

"Maybe that's why Mast had a heart attack last summer. He was trying to avoid the grass between the cracks."

"See you around. Look, don't worry. I'm sure you'll find her. Whoever-she-is is probably waiting for you right now at your place, you lucky devil—even if you are too stupid to know it."

Phil felt in his old leather case for the key Ida had given

him. He found it quickly, jangling shiny and silver among its heavier, bronze companions. At first the door stuck.

I'll just leave a note on the refrigerator. Where's a pad and pencil? Near the phone? Unwrapped cheese on the counter. Rose must have been in a hurry this morning. A letter to be mailed on the kitchen table. Ida's handwriting. Who's Menachem Baruch? Water running. The shower. "Ida? Is that you? Ida!" He headed for the bathroom, "Ida?"

The water turning off. "Hello. Just a minute." Rose swathed in towels and steam. "Oh, Phil. It's you. Let me get some clothes on."

"I'm sorry, Rose. I thought . . . Where is she? Rose? You're not at work?"

"I wasn't feeling well this morning and stayed home. Go in the kitchen. I'll be out in a second."

He sat down at the table. Calling to Rose in the bedroom, "Have you heard from her? She wasn't at the airport."

Rose's slippered feet scuffed onto the linoleum, her robe dragging. "She certainly was. Yesterday. Right on time. Where were you?" Rose wore a castle of towels on her head.

"Yesterday! But she was due today. The twelfth. Friday."

"The twelfth was *Thursday*."

His change of plans, the confusion of his flight with hers: when had Thursday become Friday? "Oh, Christ! She must have waited for me, and called."

"Can I offer you some tea?" Rose spoke in a dry tone, returning the cheese to the refrigerator.

"God, I'm sorry. I wouldn't have missed her for anything."

She put on the kettle. "But you did, didn't you?"

"Rose, I didn't mean to. I've been thinking of meeting her at the airport for the last ten days. Right in the middle of dinner, or typing my annual academic report, or looking for a tie in the closet, and suddenly there I'd be: waiting for her at the airport."

The kettle began to whistle. "Since the plane didn't land in your bedroom, it's no wonder you missed her."

"What the hell is that supposed to mean?"

"You want coffee instead? Just instant." In a level tone, "That you don't need a Ph.D. in psychology to detect avoidance."

Phil stood up and walked to the window above the sink. "Where is she now?"

"At her mother's. She didn't know what happened to you or how to find out, so she took the bus down to Manchester for the weekend."

Squeezing the bridge of his nose, "Did she leave a message for me?"

"Yes, she left the number."

He walked into the living room. The shades were half drawn, the yellow parchment like thin eyelids. He sat, fingers locked behind his neck, forearms covering his ears. Why had he missed the plane? Why hadn't he told Marge? It had never been a problem before. Why dissonance and not polyphony? Like two bands playing near each other. He couldn't follow either.

Rose came in and pulled up the shade. "Could you mail this when you leave? I told Ida I'd pick up some stamps at the hospital, but then I didn't go."

"Who's Menachem Baruch?" Phil looked at the Israeli address and imagined a dark incarnation of Paul Newman, in khaki pants and no shirt, carrying Ida through the Negev after the camel collapsed.

"Let's just say he's a man who actually got to the airport on time. A logistical giant."

"Rose, do you hate all men or just me in particular? Can't you see that I love her too?"

"What I see, Phil, is another dead end. Love? So you love her, but *I'll* be there, not you, to pick up the pieces, afterwards. You call it love? Then why does she have to shop around for someone to father her child? Or pay for it at a clinic? What are you doing with her in bed, anyway, if not that. And she won't even ask you."

Softly. "She doesn't have to ask."

"No? And you don't have to answer. Or get to the damn airport on the right day. Because I'll be there to pick her up, and to parent that child with her whether or not you father it."

"You think I wouldn't want to give her a child? And then what, disappear? Or leave my wife of fifteen years, with whose blessing I found Ida?" His eyes like marbles, "You tell me, Rose, the *right* thing to do. Nobody gets hurt. Everybody's happy. What?" The marbles were melting.

Rose walked over to him, touching his shirt. "Didn't you see any of this coming?"

"What should I have seen? That a woman sitting opposite me in a canoe would need me to father the child I never sired twenty years ago? And that I'd want to?" That the next time I looked at Marge, I'd see another face? That one plus one wouldn't equal two any more, after years of adding with the same results?

"What are you going to do, Phil?"

"What else? Go to Manchester and bring her back. Let me have the number."

Rose recited it as he began to dial. While the numbers spun, "Rose, did she find her mother?"

"Some things, I guess, you should hear from her directly."

"No, I didn't tell her. I wanted to, actually, but then I decided it would be selfish. After all, *she* never needed to know. It's my history, not hers, really. Some people need to dig, others don't."

Phil backed into the empty parking space in front of his apartment, looking over his shoulder first, then in the outside mirror. As Ida talked he thought of Mrs. Morgan, her face round and full with high cheekbones. She had been gracious when he arrived at her home in Manchester, appreciative that he'd be driving Ida back to Boston, saving her from Sunday's crowded bus.

"When I was home my mother bought some new *Haggadot*—books for the Passover holiday. I was flipping through them and remembered the part about four questions asked by four different children." Phil turned off the car, but Ida kept talking. "I always thought the main point was the recognition of elemental differences between types of people. My mother is great, but we're different types."

The engine sputtered after the key was turned off. He started the car again and gave it gas so it would shut down peacefully. "But all the types ask, don't they?" Phil tried to picture Ida as a child practicing ritual questions. "Maybe you underestimate your mother." He reached for Ida's suitcase in the back seat while opening the car door. She always packs so much, he thought, and just for a weekend with her mother this time.

"I hope you're right." Ida carried her briefcase and pocketbook. "Pretty soon she's going to need all the underestimating she can get. There's just too much in the future for me to worry about with her. I can't afford for us to miscarry over the past."

Up the cement steps. He held the front door as she started down the narrow hallway. "Then you didn't tell her about Rose yet, either." Opening the inner door over her head.

"No, I should have. I know. I've got to start preparing her. But she was so excited to see me, and it was so nice just to talk about Israel."

Phil closed the door behind him with his foot and reached for Ida with his free hand, pulling her toward him in a crunch of bodies and luggage. A breathless kiss; then another, slower, deeper. He leaned over with her, their mouths together, as she bent to release her purse and case. Finally. He'd been aching for her all the way to Connecticut, all the time chatting with her mother, all the long ride back through Ida's Israel where museums of lost scrolls and mass murder mingled with missing mothers and strange men. It had been harder to be away from her than he had anticipated.

"Just let me use the bathroom first, so we won't have to stop later." She struggled free from his embrace.

"No." Phil trembled though his words were even. Holding her head and neck with both hands, stroking her face with his thumbs. "No, Ida. Please. Leave it in your pocketbook. Come straight to bed with me."

She started to answer, but he covered her lips with his fingers.

"No. You've said everything already. I'll have to do less and less for you from now on. There's no other way. It's getting too hard. Let me this once do more, for both of us. Before you find another Menachem."

The plaster on the ceiling looked like craters on the moon. Water must have leaked through from the upper floor. He held his eyes very wide to dry. Why? Awe or fear or guilt? Old age making a surprise appearance? A preview of coming attractions?

"Ida . . ."

"Hush."

"I think my circuits are just overloaded. I must have blown a fuse."

"Sh. I'm happy just to lie here with you."

"We'll try again in a little while."

"Yes. But let me go to the bathroom, to put it in. Then you'll be fine. You're telling us both that this is rash." She sat up slowly, gathering the extra quilt around her for warmth. The white diaphragm case. Where had she left her pocketbook?

"No, Ida. Don't choose for me. Ambiguity, yes. But I still have to decide."

"You've decided." On her feet beside the bed, like a snail in a shell of blankets. "I'll be right back."

"No, Ida." He jumped up. His chest so naked without hair.

"Dear, I'm not saying . . . Maybe it's just that you haven't been with me for a while."

"But that's just it. I never left you. I was with you when I was alone, and even with Marge. Every time I closed my eyes, she was you."

When Ida tried to imagine Marge, she saw the winsome

woman from the stockings commercial. "And now that I'm *really* with you, are you with her?"

Remembering the remembering. A double exposure. Ida's brown nipples in Marge's pink.

Ida took a step closer. "Perhaps it's too crowded here for love."

"Where? In that igloo of blankets?" Phil ran his hands lightly over the cotton batting where the quilt was torn. "You look like an Eskimo, Ida." He tried to find an opening in the covers wound around her. "How about if you let me in there with you? I'll try to come alone this time." While he searched for the break in the blankets, his open lips covered Ida's. He breathed deeply into her mouth and inhaled his breath with hers. And again. No outside air between them. Ida uncrossed her hands that clutched the edges of the blanket. She let him through, folding her arms around his lower back. Within the warm tent of cloth she felt him hard against her.

That exquisite first moment when he opened her, so tight around him before she loosened up. The surprise at having been empty. That startled, sharp reminder.

And sliding together; fit, ease, follow, lead. Follow, lead. The first refrain of the rising tune. Softly, thin. A pencil outline. Follow, lead; follow, lead.

Ida thought of a baby. Those intrauterine photographs of translucent flesh against a black background, head bent, cupped hands crossed. Lit from behind, glowing around the edges of a large head. Where is the light coming from?

Follow, lead; follow, lead. Phil held her head between his hands and watched her as he leaned into her. Come with me, up the long slow circle. From tickle to ache, from front to back. Follow, lead; follow, lead.

His eyes were wide and close. From me to you, Ida. My gift. No, I to you. This time, to you, upon you. Lead, lead. "I love you, I love you," in rhythm with the thrust.

A rising spiral around a dome. White porcelain, smooth. Slip. An echo from the Holy Land, here in the holy of holies. *Kadosh, kadosh.* Follow, lead.

She tried to raise her thighs and wrap around him, to hold him deeper within, but he pinned her legs down firmly with his. Not yet; my gift. He bent forward, rubbing against her, nudging her higher. Follow, lead. A bow pulling taut, and tighter as the pitch rose. Ida looked into his eyes before she lost sight of him. All the lines in his face had fled to the corners of his eyes, leaving a smooth, placid smile. Steady, rocking. Go, I will follow you, Ida. Let the tide wash over you. Slower, larger. Don't worry, I won't stop the waves.

Kadosh, Kadosh. A rocking chair. My mother's mother's mother's mother. Here I am. *Hineini.* To pass it on. Far down at the end of a dark tunnel, a speck of light. I call to you, reach to you, flickering.

A flicker. No, not yet. Frantic, like water washing to the edge of her nose. Gasping for breath, a flutter kick to stay afloat, to catch the rising crest. Wavering. Ida surfaced again to see him whisper as he moved. "And now, and now, and now, and now." Like the sound of flint—a long, deliberate, hissing strike. Catch, and riding the swell of water. Up, up, and over upon itself. swallow Swallow SWALLOW all down the tunnel of light with the echoing voice, I am here, I am here, here, here.

And then panting on the shore. No more water, except sweat and wet legs. Her arms heavy and loose, draped over him like a damp sash. "I lost you there, toward the end. I didn't even feel you come."

"I was with *you,* too close to be seen." He rolled off and onto his side, still cradling her head in his arm.

Turning, touching his lips. "Do you think it worked?" She felt his answer on her fingertips.

"Working."

"Now? Right now? My God. The moment of life beginning."

"Beginning again."

12

The office was hardly large enough for the three of them, Ida in the swivel chair, one foot down to steady herself as she turned to face each student separately. Cora in the other chair, Melanie leaning against the file cabinet.

"No, Cora, I don't buy that. It's not just a question of relationship over rules, as you put it, because you also have a relationship with me. How do you think *I* feel, after our classes together, sharing parts of myself with you, after all, not just knowledge, but stories and feelings—and then to find this kind of cheating? It's an abrogation of our trust as well as your integrity."

Melanie ran her fingers back and forth over the rough edge where the paint had chipped off the metal file. "It didn't seem that bad at the time."

Cora's voice was higher than her friend's. "Dr. Weiss, we didn't mean anything against you personally. You know, we were out in the hall studying, just five minutes before, looking at my notes. It seemed like the same thing during the test. It was still learning, only *during* instead of *before*."

Ten yards down the hallway, a quarter of an inch on a watch—such a short distance for a moral abyss. Ida felt tired. And light, as though she couldn't get her weight down on her feet.

"Professor, Melanie has a class at three."

Ida stood up. "All right. I've already told the department

chairman that I'll be filing an unethical practice report. In addition, your grades for last term will be computed with Fs on the exam. Run along now, or you'll be late. Let's see that this type of thing never happens again."

After Melanie left, Cora waited near the door. "Could I ask you, do letters have to go out to parents? I mean, it doesn't matter for me. My Mom knows and all, but Melanie . . ."

"Cora, who copied from whom?" Ida sat down again.

"You see, it won't do Melanie any good for her father to find out. She's so afraid of him."

"She copied from you, didn't she?"

Cora nodded in response.

"And of course you knew."

Another nod. "I shouldn't be telling you this, but Melanie's father, well, he's hit her before. Not like a spanking, you know, but bad. If you send that letter, it won't help Melanie."

"And what about you, Cora? Is this friendship helping you? Are you even helping Melanie, really?"

Cora pulled at the rings in her spiral notebook. "I know I did wrong. I'm sorry. I won't do it again. But can you please just not send the letter?"

A knock on the half-open door. Then two faster taps. Mast poked his head around and peeked in. "Am I interrupting?" Cora walked out backwards. "No, I was just leaving anyway. Thanks, Professor Weiss. If there's anything I can do . . ." Cora nearly collided with Mast, who posed like a bullfighter by the door, which he whipped to the side as Cora passed.

"Whew! A hot one?" He shook his hand sideways, limp at the wrist. "I brought you the unethical practice forms. Was that the culprit?"

"Presumably."

Off the top of the bookcase Mast picked up Ida's copy of the Monet catalog from the Fine Arts Museum. "Did they own up to it?"

"In a way. They admit to having done it but question if it's wrong, or how wrong. They expect absolutes, not a continuum, you know? Gray isn't bad because it isn't black or white."

He stopped flipping the pages. "Um, just love those poppies." Closing the book, "Sure. I tell them, you think it's black and white, at opposite ends of the field. All the scoring in the end zone. But in real life the tough calls—all the calls, actually—are on the fifty yard line. Very little ever happens in the end zone. Moral choices are made in the middle."

"Good, Arnold. I'll keep that in mind if I ever catch any jocks cheating." She glanced at her watch. The hands a perfect right angle, the midday L that always promised not to move. Plenty of time before her mother's bus at 4:30. Ida wondered if she could squeeze in a nap before four, in the ladies' lounge. "Incidentally, is there any way I can file these reports without a letter going home?"

Mast was rotating his wedding ring around under its hairy wreath. "Beats me. It's an automatic procedure once you submit the violation notice. Why do you ask?"

Ida kept looking at the 3:00 L. 9:00 to 3:00, the sturdy bookends of the day, back to back. Now with just a little nap somewhere in between . . .

"Hi Arnold. Ida, can I speak to you?" Phil addressed Ida in his school voice, all the syllables on the same note except *da* and *you*. The restricted range of considered opinions and prolonged deliberations. But his face was flushed. "Look, your phone's off the hook."

"Hello, Phil." Her measured response. "Yes, I had a sticky conference with some students and didn't want to be disturbed."

Mast stayed.

Phil paused, but Ida helped him. "Did you finish that article you wanted me to proof?"

"Yes, but if you're busy now . . ."

Mast accompanied them part of the way to Phil's office. Then Ida went on with Phil; though she walked quickly, she was a half step behind. "I think Mast wonders if you're making some kind of move on me. He's always trying to pin down whether I'm single or . . ."

Phil took Ida's elbow and sidestepped into an empty classroom.

"Hey, what's . . ."

"Ida, Rose tried to call you but couldn't get through. She's gone to Brigham and Women's. Started bleeding last night . . ."

Ida returned to the desk where the nurse had first told her to take a seat since Ms. Grandby was down in Emergency. But Ida hadn't found Rose in the emergency room.

"Miss Weiss, you weren't supposed to go down there." In starched, white syllables.

"Doctor."

"Pardon me?"

"*Doctor* Weiss." Pronounced in stainless steel.

The nurse opened a ledger and kept her eyes lowered. "Are you involved in Ms. Grandby's case?"

"Not medically."

"Hm. Perhaps they've sent her to one of the holding rooms. I'll check. Could you please wait here this time?"

I should have called home yesterday. Just to check in. She's alone there so often when I'm with Phil. Ida paced between the elevator doors on waxed tiles the color of olive pits. I never even let her know this time I wouldn't be home. What if my mother had called and . . . Mother! Oh, God! At the bus station. Ida looked at the bulging cornea of the clock over the nursing station. 4:45. She's been there fifteen minutes already, steaming about how I'm always late. "Excuse me, is there a pay phone on the floor?" If only Phil hasn't left his office yet. A 3:30 meeting with the dean, some appointments with students . . .

"Phil. Oh thank heavens! I forgot about my mother. Could you page her at the Greyhound station, tell her to wait, and go get her? The 2:30 bus out of Hartford. . . . No, don't bring her to my house. Why would you have a key? Maybe to dinner. Pretend I'm meeting her there. . . . If I can. . . . Brown's, sure. That's good. Just say I got held up, or something. . . . No, I haven't seen her yet. They won't tell me anything. They're trying to *find* her! . . . Oh, and Phil, remember, I never told my mother Rose was pregnant. . . . Yes, I can call you at the restaurant if I don't manage to meet you there. Say I got stuck in traffic or something."

Ida walked a short way down the hall, looking in the rooms. White draped metal beds on wheels, one-legged tables on casters, portable utility carriages, mobile aluminum poles—coat racks for plastic I.V. bags. All gliding on clean floors, shining like wet ice. Ida felt sweaty behind the knees. She leaned against the wall, looking into one of the rooms on a slant. Just tilt this place for a second, and everything will roll out the doors.

"Dr. Weiss?"

"Yes, right here."

"Ms. Grandby is down at the end, in room 411."

A large room, partitioned by pale yellow curtains hanging from tracks on the ceiling. Rose sat on the far cot, staring out the window. A faded green hospital robe, tied at the back, barely reached around. She turned to Ida, her eyes like the inside of conch shells. The white going pink with the sound of the ocean.

Shaking her head, "It's gone." Gone before it arrived, before I really believed it was there. An upset stomach, tender breasts. Like a low-grade infection I couldn't shake. "Maybe it was never really a baby, but just clots."

"Oh, Rose." Not to cry. It won't help her if I cry, too. "Why?"

Rose wiped her eyes on a snowball of Kleenex. "They don't know. It happens sometimes in the early months. Maybe a defect." From the bed frame an angular light fixture reached toward her on a skeletal arm, bent at the elbow. "A spontaneous abortion, they say. *Spontaneous*. As though anything about that child was spontaneous." *Aborted*—shades of murder and space shots canceled for inclement weather. "Would I abort a baby I chose!" Chosen, unlike the mindless accidents that happen to millions of housewives. All those unwanted third children. And fourths.

Ida put both arms around Rose's head and closed her eyes in the bouquet of blond curls. "Why didn't you call me, last night?"

"I phoned the doctor. He said it might be nothing, that I should come in tomorrow if the bleeding didn't stop. In the morning it did stop, but the cramps continued, and then in the afternoon . . . Besides, I kept thinking of getting you out of bed, and . . ." Interrupting, a sin her mother had always abhorred. Don't interrupt, Rose. There's a circle around you that's yours. Stay in it. "And what could you do, really?" Rose slipped out from under the ring of Ida's arms and took one hand.

"Rose, you can try again, right?"

Right. More appointments. More instruments and ointment. Stirrups. Thermometers and waiting rooms and payment in advance. "Ida, it's never going to work. I know it." And my weight and my blood pressure and my age. My fault. Unworthy. The angel will whisper in someone else's ear: *You're* pregnant, not her. White-robed Gabriel with multicolored wings, singing in church but not to me.

"When I was little and lost my first tooth, the tooth fairy forgot to come. I just lay awake half the night listening to my father getting drunk downstairs." One tooth after another.

"Mrs. Grandby?" A nurse walked in quickly, speaking too loudly. "How are you feeling now? I'm going to give you a shot; it'll just make you a little drowsy, help you relax." The end of the stethoscope bobbed from the pocket of a white polyester pants suit. "There. We'll come to get you for the D and C in about fifteen minutes."

"Are you sure we have to do this? We couldn't just wait a few days and see?"

"No, it's just to guard against infection. Make sure all the tissue is out."

Tissue.

Flesh and blood. A mind? As smart as a dog? A hamster? Mourning the death of a gerbil. "Rose, I'm not sure how to say this, or if this is the right time, but you know, we would have raised two children together. If not two, then one. We'll parent our child together, whichever one of us can have it."

Rose poured a glass of water from the plastic woodgrain pitcher near the bed. She drank it slowly. "No. It would be like loving someone else's child. It would be, well, unbalanced. Your baby, made out of you."

"Rose, neither of *my* parents made me." We'd be together for the birth, and teething, first words and first steps. "It's *deciding* to have children, wanting them, helping someone else want them, that matters. If you hadn't, I might never . . ."

Rose looked at Ida, so thin, even in her coat, which she hadn't taken off. We eat together, the same meals—but she's slim and I gain. "It isn't perfect, Ida." It isn't fair!

You want perfect, kill yourself and go to heaven. "Rose, what would you say if this had happened to me? It could, you know. We're neither of us that young any more. I need you, Rose. We need each other."

Now, but in a year, or two, or five? When the next Phil Manning comes along—a single, Jewish one? Demoted to Auntie Rose. "Now."

"All thens turn into nows."

An orderly appeared with a wheelchair. He stooped to open the metal footrests.

Rose snapped, "I don't need that. Really, I can . . ."

"I know, dear, but it's the rules. The same for everyone." Brightly, "I just wheeled a young man out to his car. Feeling fine. An appendectomy nearly a week ago."

"But you don't take out everyone's appendix, do you?"

Ida spotted her mother and Phil in the back booth at the restaurant. Two dull figures against the resonant red—crimson vinyl benches, red and black carpeting, velvety rose walls. Like the inside of some great, sanguine organ. Why don't they call it Red's instead of Brown's?

Phil saw her from his seat and walked over to the doorway. Mrs. Morgan was facing the other direction, her back to the front door.

The dread of words, of saying it to him. Dead. A thin wedge of nausea and then another slice of dread—explaining to her mother. Ida felt cold and sweaty under her coat.

Stumbling through it. Go now. Too hard to do both together. This evening, Yes. Late. Call. We'll see. I'll go back and bring Rose home right after I take Mother to the airport. Go, it's okay. I'll make apologies, tell her you had to hurry back to a meeting.

Mrs. Morgan sat close to the wall, leaving enough room on her bench for three other people. Ida slid over to the middle on the opposite side of the table.

"Ida dear, you look just awful. How's Rose? Whatever has happened?"

Ida stared at her mother's hair, straight on top where the hat had flattened it, little curls around the temples. "Mother, Rose had a miscarriage."

Mildred gasped. "My God, I didn't even think she . . . But you never mentioned a boyfriend." Pushing away the cup of soup she had been nursing, "Under the circumstances, I guess it's a blessing. How is she feeling?"

The waitress hovered impatiently. Ida ordered a Coke.

"Is that all you're having? Ida, I do worry about your eating habits. Why don't you try some soup?"

"Mother, there's no boyfriend, and it's not a blessing. Rose wanted to have a baby." Ida thought about going to the bathroom. Or making a phone call. Maybe a car would smash into hers, parked at the curb, and she'd be called outside to examine the damage. Exchange addresses, wait for the policeman. Later, the conversation with her mother could slip by more easily, like soft-boiled eggs, cooled.

"But what do you mean no boyfriend?"

"There are ways today, Mother. In a doctor's office."

Mrs. Morgan remembered Rose last August, sitting in the armchair. In the living room, when she'd stopped in Manchester with Ida on the way to Boston. Level-headed Rose, helping Ida move. Sipping tea while Ida looked in the attic for some spare sheets to fit a twin bed. Rose, speaking softly about Ida's pain, and strength. Mrs. Morgan had thought Ida was in good hands. "How selfish of her! Did she think of her family, how her mother would feel, or you, Ida, to impose this sort of thing on you . . ."

Ida held a piece of ice between her teeth as the Coke sloshed around in the glass. Cold, like that snowy night in December, dancing with Rose in the street when they first knew. Drinking eggnog, and Rose's Christmas songs on the stereo. The white amaryllis on the coffee table. They harmonized on old camp songs and grammar school hymns sung before assemblies. A-bun-dance of glad-ness on meee He-ee be-ee-stows.

"Or even the baby, with no father. And trying to raise a child alone these days, did she ever give any thought to that?" Rose was so solid, Mrs. Morgan thought. So heavy in the armchair, an anchor for Ida.

"She isn't exactly alone."

"Ida, on a day like this, eating ice! Get something warm, won't you?" Mrs. Morgan checked her watch. "Just to think of Rose, a single woman with a child. You know, Ida, back in the days before we adopted you, I'd sometimes see a teenage girl with her baby. I wanted a child so badly then. And I'd think of those young girls in trouble—what should have been the joy of their lives, instead . . . Timing is everything in life."

"But Rose isn't sixteen, Mother. Listen, I've got to go soon, back to the hospital. I can drive you to the airport, and . . ."

"Oh, no, dear. I'll take a cab. You get back to her. Yes, I didn't realize she'd still be there, in the hospital, I mean." Mrs. Morgan looked for the compact in her purse. "I guess this visit was a mistake. For such a short time, it was really silly. And I just saw you last weekend. But we had such a nice visit, and when I realized I'd save money on the Houston flight by leaving from Boston rather than Hartford, and I could take the bus straight down here—see you and Pearl, both of my girls for the price of one, well I . . ."

"It's all right, Mom."

"And your friend having to drive over to meet me. I feel so badly. You shouldn't have troubled him, such a nice man. Perhaps he and his wife know a nice single fellow they could introduce you to. Sometimes you have to ask, Ida. You don't have to be embarrassed."

"Oh, Mother."

"Ida, about Rose, I just want you to know . . ."

"Mother, look, let's talk about it another time." Why don't they bring the check!

"No, I want to say this. You know, each life has its own rewards. You have had a very rough time, don't think I don't know that. And now Rose . . . well, you girls both have your careers. And that's something. When your father died, I wished I had some work to carry me along, but then I thought, I've got my family. It's no good to be wanting more than you're due."

"Due? Mother, who's keeping score? Do you think Rose isn't entitled to a child because she has a job? What does one thing have to do with the other?" God, where is that waitress!

"Well, take Pearl, for instance. Don't you think she gets to feeling trapped in the house with the baby? I know how you must see it, when you can't have one of your own, but look at it from the other side: day after day, diapers and formula, day after day. It all works out for the best. You have your teaching, and we all have little Artie."

"*We* don't have him, Mother. Pearl has him, you have him. I don't. Yes, as a nephew, but not a son, or grandson. It's not the same. Working isn't enough for a life. It's no substitute."

"Here's your check, ladies. I'm sorry to keep you waiting. Terrible weather, isn't it? So gray."

"Yes, thank you. Ida, I'll take that." Opening her beige wallet, "Things are so expensive in the city. I always forget." Mildred handed the waitress a ten-dollar bill. "Ida, I know you're upset about Rose now, but you'll calm down later and think about it. A person can't just decide for themselves. What would they think at work about what she was doing? Have you considered that? You can't buck the whole world. Society has reasons for these things."

"And we have reasons, too."

"Ida, it's arrogant, to think you can run everything by

yourself. Rose has no right to take matters into her own hands this way. Some things should be left to God. So to speak."

"And how do you know you speak for God, Mother? Are you so sure you're right?"

"Are you so sure *you* are? She is?" Mrs. Morgan stood beside the coat rack at the corner of the booth. "Ida, you've always been so headstrong. Always making up your mind. I used to say to your father, 'Art, she's too willful.' The world is full of doubt, Ida. Mostly doubt. There are so few things in life that can bear decisions."

Ida looked at her mother poised above her, tall in her tailored, tweed coat. Balanced evenly on two feet in that peculiar, face front position she always assumed before walking. So she had stood on the threshold of Ida's childhood, reading to her and Pearl. Not sitting on their beds. Standing. Hickory Dickory Dock. Posed like the Greek chorus figures, before contrapposto.

"I hope you listen to me, Ida. For once."

13

"So then, after I stagger over to the phone, who is it? Mitzi Braiman." In falsetto, " 'Yes, Doctor. No Doctor. So sorry to bother you at home.' She just can't decide between Psych 203 and Introductory Physics. Do I care? Yes, Mitzi dear. If I weren't so smashed I'd have told her, go fuck yourself, Mitzi darling. As your adviser, I'd be delighted to sign the papers."

Mast chuckled at his younger colleague's repartee. "Oh, Ida, come join us. We're swapping stories. What's the dirt on your cheaters? You know, I once had a dullard who was so 'clever' he actually plagiarized from my own book and then tried to deny it!"

Ida glanced around the faculty lounge. "Hi, Arnold, Mitch. I was just looking for Phil Manning. He borrowed my *Norton Anthology of Modern Drama*, and I need it now. But I guess he's not here. Have you seen him?"

Mitch straddled the chair as though riding a horse. "Now *there's* a smart man, Phil Manning. He's leaving this whole act behind. No more bullshit papers and multiple guess exams. No more Mitzi Braiman at 11:30 p.m. Two years in L.A. care of C.S.A.C. Can you beat that? What do those guys call research for twenty grand a year? How about, 'the sociological implications of skimpy bathing attire.' I'd go for that."

The door was ajar, but his office was empty. Ida walked gingerly to the desk. He never filed anything, just made piles. Underneath the stapler: a manila envelope, not unsealed but torn open. Ida removed the cover letter. Across the letterhead, THE CENTER FOR THE STUDY OF AMERICAN CULTURE. Below, "Dear Professor Manning: We are pleased to inform you that you have been selected as one of twelve recipients of the National I. F. Fortmus Grants for Advanced Sociological Research. Our panel was most impressed with your proposal, and we look forward in the coming year to . . ."

Ring, Ring. Muffled, as though under water. Ring, ring. Ida looked for the phone. Not on the bookcase, the filing cabinet. Ring, ring. The cord running along the floor, up the front of the desk, disappearing into a drawer. Open it, ring, as though the gray desk had swallowed it. Jonah calling from inside the whale. "Hello? . . . Phil, yes, but how did you know I'd be here, and why the hell are you keeping the phone inside a drawer? . . . But what good will that do? You can still hear it. Either unplug it or . . . Phil, I found this letter, and Mitch mentioned . . . Next year, why didn't you tell me? I didn't even know you applied! . . . But . . . Phil, we've got to talk. . . . No . . . All right. When will you be back from your conference?"

Ida pushed away the pillow and laid her face flat on the mattress, trying to keep her head in line with her body. Her earliest memory was resting like this, in a crib. The soft sheet pulled tight. Then wet against her cheek, drooling down her mouth. Turn the other cheek. Always dry and warm at first, then wet. Turn, turn; no more dry.

Or turning her head on the beach blanket, facing to the side, warm sand ribbed beneath her stomach. Rob leaning over her, the hair from his chest brushing lightly against her back as he rubbed oil on her shoulders and legs. The salty smell in stiff towels. Rob drying her after a bath, Rob reading his article to her as she stretched across the bed, Rob mowing the lawn in the rain. Laughing, kissing, the smell of cut grass in his hair. Rob, where are you? And the sun and the oil and the wet grass?

Ida squeezed her eyes tight and turned her head toward the wall, edging down further in the bed for a dry patch of sheet. Just to be asleep, glorious sleep, warm and safe and dark. Asleep, where Rob and Phil could not leave her; deep sleep, down below the ripples of nausea and oily patches of Melanie's father floating on the surface.

She heard the refrigerator door close, water running in the sink. Rose must be up, too.

No, better try to sleep. I have to teach tomorrow. If I don't sleep, I'll even be robbed of the morning. Mornings, strong and sated with sleep. Scrambled eggs and bouncy steps and pictures in the *Globe* of footed baby nighties, flowered flannel. Special clearance, two for one. The day passes and the sleep drips out, a slow leak. Tired at noon, wavering. And then the evenings, a rising tide of fear. Images of Aunt Grace at Passover, oh Gracie dear. Yes, we all know. Over there. In maternity clothes. Sh. Mildred is just beside herself. And on purpose, she says. God only knows. And not yet divorced, officially. Sh. Mildred's just sick about it. Unstable, she thinks. Despite the degrees and jobs, Ida was never really . . .

The clink of a spoon inside a glass. Duddle duddle duddle duddle. Rose must be making chocolate milk.

Time to sleep. It's getting too late. Ida turned her head again, straightening her arms at her sides, palms up. Trying to replace shallow breathing with deep, rhythmic breaths. In, out out out. In, out out out. First it was too late to have a baby, then too late not to have a baby. Happening without me, through me. Growing inside regardless of what I think, or what my mother thinks, or what Arnold Mast says to Mitch Breslau. Well, she didn't *come* here pregnant. It would have shown earlier. She could at least *call* herself Mrs. Who'd question it? The dean feels, you know, in front of the students and all . . . And the image, public relations-wise. I don't know. Is that legal? Hey, do you think it's one of *us*, the father? Anyone we know?

Quiet down! It's too noisy here to sleep. Ida tried the pillow again. Phil? Where are you? To cuddle me and cover my ears, and bring me some chocolate milk. Too busy editing the paper for the conference you forgot to tell me about. Publication deadlines, deadlines for the abstract. Dead lines. Like your phone in the desk. Hidden away, or out of town. Out.

Ida sat up. The hell with it! "Rose? Whatever you're eating in there, make it double for me." All this talking going on anyway, it might as well be firsthand.

2:00 a.m.

"Ida, I watch myself eating a meal in the middle of the night, like if I nurture myself enough . . . when I know it's the opposite, not good for myself, less chance for a baby. Chance. We add up a lifetime of choices and call it chance."

"And now, suddenly, I'm thinking about Rob all the time. You know, Rose, Phil was like a pearl, soft and smooth all around the raw stone. He muted the pain. But now I hurt for two. Loss and loss."

"Or I think maybe I should adopt Cecily, you remember, the child from the institute with spina bifida. They bring her to the hospital—I see her twice a week. She has nothing, no family, no home. Who will take her? I at least love her and could care for her. But then I wonder if that's fair either, to me, to you. Am I deluding myself into a consolation prize, like getting a puppy instead of a baby? And then when she's grown, and never grows up. Why not adopt someone from the old age home? Right? And the expense, too."

"I needed all my courage to decide yes. No looking back. But now that it's done, happening by itself from now on, I can afford to see all the problems, all the hesitancies, terrors. They hover around like vultures whenever I get tired. The baby makes me tired all the time."

3:00 a.m.

"Choice, Rose? Grand old Rose, nearly omnipotent. You really think you did it *all* yourself? *Your* fault your father was drunk all the time, right? Must have been something *you* did. And your weight, the glandular problem. Nothing metabolic going on? For that matter, why doesn't Cecily just go fix her spine? It's her body, right? Don't some people walk on burning coals? Maybe we can even defy death?"

"Ida, you don't even get mad at them. '*Poor* Phil, what else can he do?' The honorable Phil, choosing the devoted wife! The poor dear, two loves are ripping him apart. And poor Rob, the victim of his parents' values and his reflexive rebellions. You helped him choose the beautiful, rich lawyer, to spare him the eternal conflict. You need to kick them in the balls, Ida. To be angry enough to reject them. In a way, you're as emotionally dependent as your sister Pearl."

4:00 a.m.

"Tomorrow, Ida—well, I guess it's already today—let's sign up for childbirth classes. No, better, we can audit the one that's already meeting in the evening at the hospital. It's a little early—they usually wait until the last months of pregnancy, but when you're as late as we are, you need a head start. And you haven't even been to the doctor! You might need vitamins or something. Make the appointment, and I'll go with you."

"Rose, when you're ready to give up, we'll know it. In the meantime, let's not-give-up together. Back to the infertility clinic, and tomorrow we start the New-and-Improved-Morgan-Grandby-Fitness-Center. Do-it-yourself in your own home. You need the diet, I need the exercise. Rose, you know, I thought of a name last night, if it's a girl. Orna. I met a child in Israel with that name, on the kibbutz. It means 'light,' actually 'a pleasing light.' *Or* is light. Orna Lee, 'my gentle light.' "

"Orna Lee Morgan? Morgan-Weiss?"

"Morgan-Grandby."

"I'm touched, Ida, I really am, but we need fewer names, not more. Simplicity, not complication."

"That may be, but it's not what we've got. Ours are the problems of more, not less. We've chosen them. 'You can't choose *not* to have problems, just which problems to have.' Remember when you told me that?"

5:00 a.m.

"And what about if you marry again, or should I say when?"

"I hope it's *when*, Rose, I really do. But not tomorrow. Whatever happens, I just have to have faith we'll work it out. Joint custody, huh? Sarah Stevens at work says that's the only good part about divorce. Some time with, some time away."

"I won't divorce you, Ida, even if you do marry again. Kill you, maybe, but no divorce."

"I know. Extended family—the best antidote for divorce."

"Faith is a good thing, Ida. And since I can't quite drum it up for the angel Gabriel any more, I guess we can pin those peacock wings on Orna's future. Hail the angelic wingspread!"

"To Orna, whoever she may be."

"Come on, Mama. I'll get you some more milk and we'll toast to Orna."

"Hey, it's already morning. Time to say the *Sh'ma*."

"What?"

"Never mind. How many glasses of chocolate milk does this make, anyway? Let's raise the fourth glass."

The window was open in the associate dean's office. "Just can't seem to regulate the heat. To keep the girls in the outer room warm, it's got to be sweltering in here, and when I open the window to breathe a little, it sets off the thermostat and turns this place into an oven so I have to open the window more! You can't win. What can I do for you?"

Ida stood near the bookcase to avoid the blast of cold air. "I'd like to see the letter regarding cheating that's being sent to the father of my student, Melanie Smithson."

Dean Grey shuffled through the papers on his desk. "Well you know, Ida, it's just a form letter. One's just like the next."

"Yes, but sometimes a personal note can be more effective, don't you think?"

The dean buzzed his secretary to ask if the forms had already gone out. As he waited, he kept the receiver on his ear and spoke to Ida as though she were on the phone. "Well, of course, you could always write an additional letter of your own to this gentleman. You see, there's always the danger that the formal notice could get lost if we let all the professors take them and add—yes, Donna, are you there?"

Ida sidestepped, "Is there a second call coming through? Look, the other light on your phone is flashing."

"No, that's just . . . Damned heat! Now it's getting chilly." The dean tried to hammer the window closed with his fist.

"Listen, Dave, let me go speak to Donna directly. I'll follow up on the mailing end of things, in any case."

In the outer waiting room, Donna had located the letter. "Are you sure the dean approved your taking this? You know, I'm the one who's ultimately accountable for all correspondence . . ."

"Don't worry, Donna. You're off the hook on this one. I've got it." Ida spoke while checking her mailbox. The pink slip for a phone message lay in the bottom.

Time: 9:15 a.m.
Date: Feb. 20
Message for: I. M. W.
Won't be in today. Sprained ankle.
Can you collect my mail?
P. M.

Dear Mom,

I know there's something terribly cowardly about breaking this to you in

No. Why am I always apologizing? If I didn't think this were the best way, I'd . . .

Since I won't be home till Passover, there's no way I can tell you in person, and by that time you'd probably see just by looking before I'd have the chance to

Terrific! In this letter she'd also know before I managed to tell her.

Ida put down her writing pad and picked up the scissors again. All around her on the bed were piles of photographs sorted by category—Florida Trip with Rose, Israel Vacation, Maine with Phil. Propped against the wall was a large posterboard covered with overlapping pictures. Ida had just taped a four inch border of blue cardboard all around the edges of the old collage.

Damn!

While she was trying to write, the Elmer's glue had been oozing onto the bedspread.

Ida carefully cut around the outline of the Dome of the Rock. She held it against the right side of the montage. Good, a little white here to balance Artie's diapers on the other side.

Dear Mom,

Sometimes when a person tells me something, I wish I

had known earlier so that first I could assimilate it myself before I had to

Projection. Pure projection. That's me, not her. Talk to *her*.

Back to the scissors. Rose in Front of Our New House. Cut off that dying shrub at the side. Good. The porch looks better that way.

Rose stood in the bedroom doorway. "How long have you been at this?"

"Oh, I didn't hear you come in. Well, seven years I guess."

"No, silly. I meant how long today? This room looks like you've been playing hooky."

"Yes, Mommy, I'm so sorry, I'll never do it again."

Rose walked into the room and examined the poster. "So that's how you do it, adding on from the outside."

"Like a tree."

At the center were wedding shots and Rob sitting on a beach. "Look, Ida, the farther you go from the middle, the more pictures there are of you."

"That's because in the beginning I was always behind the camera. Rob never could take pictures, even with the Instamatic I had before I bought the one with the better lens." Ida started on the snapshots of Malka as Rose went to change her clothes.

Dear Mom,

I'm telling you in a letter because it's so private—almost too private for words. Rose knows, of course, but otherwise I wanted you to really hear it first.

Split infinitive. And to think I teach English! Should I write from my happiness or to her fear?

I know you'll be upset initially, but try to see it from

Nobody died, Mom. For God's sake! It's done. We can bless it or . . .

"Ida, can you hear me from in there? I saw a robin today on the way home from work."

Ida pushed aside the pad, pictures replacing the words in her mind. She smiled at Menachem slouching in front of the Western Wall. Better cut out some of that foreground or it will dwarf him. Rose came back and sat on the bed.

"I always do it in the spring, it seems." Ida pasted down a loose corner of the nun standing with the tour guide on the steps of *Yad Vashem*. "I start to worry that I'll lose some of the rolls of film before I get a chance to go through them and separate what I want to keep. Once the pictures are glued down and lacquered, they're mine."

"And then?"

"And then, up it goes on the wall for another year." Ida stood and backed away to view the collage from a distance. "You hold it up for me. I can't seem to get far enough away to see if it hangs together. Would you add some more shots on the top?"

"Not unless you're going to frame it."

"No. No more frames, or glass. It's getting too big."

The photo of Phil was cut at the waist so that only the handlebars showed of the bike he was sitting on. "I like that one of Phil. I have to admit it, Ida. You really catch him there. Tell me, how's his leg?"

"It doesn't seem to be healing. Now they're talking about setting it in some kind of soft cast. He's in pain whenever he walks, but traction's not right for it either. I'll probably go over tonight and bring him dinner. Depending on how I'm feeling." Ida knocked on her stomach. "Hey, little one, you hungry in there? Whatever you're doing, it sure makes *me* tired. Too tired."

"How about *I'll* make dinner." Rose gathered up the glue and spare picture clippings. "You've even got time for a nap before supper. I'll call you when I'm ready."

Dear Mom,
It says, "Choose life." I had to. Please trust me, I know that if we just

The elliptical approach. She'll hate it.

React, relax, regress. I do it out of stress. I just need some time to rethink things. Or stop thinking about them.

So his wife is coming up for a few weeks. So? She's worried about his leg, wants to help take care of him. Well, maybe it will give me a rest, emotionally. At least I won't be wondering yes or no, if I'll see him or not. He's hardly in school any more. In and out, just for his classes. Sleeping a lot, from the painkillers. And the pain.

Good, Rose isn't home yet. I'm too tired to talk about it. Too tired to frame it in words, hang it on the wall, can't miss it there. Before it's said I can still fold it up, hide it away in a drawer.

It probably will be easier not to see him for a few weeks, anyway, since I don't know when he'll reach for me and when . . . And besides, I don't stay over any more. A phased withdrawal. And I'm hardly in the mood these days, for that or . . . Just for sleep, oblivion. The only cure for nausea. But it's so hard to sleep.

I'll pull down the shades in the room. The light bothers my eyes. And get Rose's down comforter. She won't mind. Been warm all day, but now . . .

Refrain, rename; rewrite, respite.

I didn't think it would happen this fast. I always knew in time, that in time he'd not be there, but I thought that at least for another year, at least for the baby's birth. Maybe it's better this way, to start next year new, without.

Since Rose isn't home yet, maybe I'll just . . . Just for a while. In the closet it will be dark enough. Just roll up the blanket in a ball. Umm. Round and round. Nice. It might look strange to someone else, but no one's here, and if it makes me feel better for a little while, in the closet, down on the floor with nowhere to fall, so what? Just this once. And I'll bring some chocolate. A better taste in my mouth. Now, just close the door. Hard to get a grip on it from the inside. Umm. Reminds me of when I used to play hide-and-seek. The best part. When I hear Rose drive up, I'll come out. I can hear when she opens the front door. Can I hear that from in here? Maybe I'll be able to doze off a little.

Regressive, recessive. Relapse, recede, rehash, review. Renew.

Ida lay in the back of the car, staring at the metal rim where the window met the spongy ceiling, dotted with little holes like a pincushion. She didn't want to go to the childbirth class, not even as an "auditor," in Rose's words. She was too tired at night. Maybe they could find one that met in the morning. Rose's car jiggled as she drove, the springs in the seat squeaking in time. Like birds cheeping in a nest.

"I can exercise at home, Rose. Why do I have to do leg lifts in a group? Childbirth is not a team sport, you know." Ida crawled out of the back seat on all fours, swinging her feet around only at the last minute. "We could buy a Lamaze book and practice together, in private." She trudged along like a bear cub behind its mother.

"Why don't your students just stay home for college? Save thousands of dollars and study in their bedrooms. Reading's not a group sport either." Rose led Ida down the familiar corridors. "Remind me to stop by my station afterwards. I left some charts I want to review for tomorrow."

They walked by a pregnant woman standing with her husband at a drinking fountain. "They'll think we're lesbians, Rose. Maybe we should tell them you had a sex change operation just after fathering the child."

"Stop it, Ida. I don't know why you're getting all worked up about this. I spoke to the woman who heads it, and she was very receptive. She says it's a support group, not just sessions in directed breathing. Ah, here it is."

Ida looked through the glass in the upper part of the

door. "I can breathe without directions." A dozen women were lying on colored mats, propped up against a motley crew of men tickling their mates' bloated abdomens. "Oh Rose, please. Let's go home. I can tell this isn't for me. I could never stand these mind-over-matter yoga things. I'm not the true believer type. It's all metaphor to me. Otherwise, I'd just trust in God to take away my pain."

Rose opened the door.

"Or the Holy Ghost, or massive doses of vitamin E, astral projection, or self-hypnosis."

"Now exhale, two, three, four. *Effleurage*, two, three, four." To the tune of a Brahms waltz. "Good, very good." The instructor snapped off the phonograph. "Okay, let's form a circle now and get on to sharing."

"Rose, this looks like a taping for *Mister Roger's Neighborhood*. That's why they sit on the floor."

"We have some visitors with us this evening, Ida Morgan and her partner Rose Grandby. Rose, Ida, come over and join us in the circle, won't you? I'm Lil, by the way. Your instructor. We'll have everyone say their names tonight before they speak. Rose and Ida aren't regulars, it's too early in the pregnancy ordinarily, but they wanted to see what we do here. Rose is a physical therapist on staff at the hospital." Ida explained that her back was hurting and she'd prefer not to sit on the floor, but the circle politely formed close to her chair, including her in the arc.

"After our warm-ups, when we don't have a guest lecturer on some medical aspect of pregnancy, we usually have a good news/bad news session. Everyone must say something, even if only a few words. Suzi, you're always pretty verbal—why don't you get the ball rolling."

The good news was that Mrs. Hortonstein had decided not to stay at her daughter-in-law's for a week after the baby was born; that Maalox did work for heartburn; that Joan Something was having twins, as confirmed by ultrasound, and you could now get copies of the internal pictures without bribing the technician; that the hospital had approved procedures to waive required check-ins the night before Cesarean sections if both husband and wife signed affidavits testifying that the patient had not eaten after midnight; that the woman with blond pigtails above her ears had stopped dreaming of slaughtered kittens; that the fetal movements of Elwin Junior (gender confirmed by amniocentesis) reminded Junior's mother of the mediation between inner and outer life—herself as a semipermeable membrane with life on either side, hers as well as his, and that perhaps life itself was a flimsy tissue between the halves of the vast unknown, before and after; that Edward and Karena had decided not to get married until after the baby's birth to verify in their own minds whether love or guilt was their true motivation; that Josh had agreed on a cleaning lady once a week; that soft-spoken Carma or Carla or Carra was reinstated in her job after winning her appeal that mandatory maternity leave was a violation of federal law; that donors of mother's milk could now be paid for their services; that the milkmobile would make home pickups; and that Lenore finally told her mother she was expecting, after realizing her secrecy had been prompted by the fear of a third miscarriage.

Ida shook her head, and Rose said the good news was that she and Ida had found the group. Ida stopped listening when they started around again and the kitten killer began talking about motherhood as a subsidiary of childhood. Ida's good news was that finally and forever the fear was gone, the word *barren*—a life sentence, stricken from the record. A last-minute reprieve. Not a punishment from on high. *She* had chosen—a child, grandchildren. A decision for all eternity. And also red Stride Rite shoes, the P.T.A., and the "*Ma Nishtana*." The whys that elicit stories, "why is it different," from generation to generation. "*V'shenantam levanecha*" (and you shall teach it to your children).

"My name is Eilene Macintosh. Sorry, I forgot to mention it when we went around with the good news. My bad news is sickness, all the time, hour after hour. Someday this swelling will be a baby, but now it's just a giant virus."

And the good news is that Rose can take her summer vacation in October, followed by an extra month's leave of absence, to stay home with the baby. Then I'll be off most of December and January for midsemester break. The courses I can teach beforehand, this summer, will supplement our income, and if I apply for a research grant for the following year . . .

"But now that Mother Hortonstein isn't coming, I'll have the new baby to take care of plus Josie and Missy. Jim's mother is no help, but neither is he, and we can't exactly hire a nurse after we got rid of his mother by arguing that I like to do everything myself."

And Rose has a friend who's giving up her *au pair*, a Swiss girl who wants to stay in the States until her parents come in the summer. We can convert the den into her bedroom, and since classes end in April now that they instituted a study week before finals . . .

"The worst news is that now, with little sexual interest on my part, I realize how much of it was physical all along, and how little else there is. He looks so, so flat to me. He hardly talks—reminds me of a potted plant at times, I swear, and I feel terrible saying this to you, when next week Jim will be back here again, but . . ."

I hardly show yet. Probably won't have to face that

until next year. The new students in September will *meet* me pregnant, it will seem natural to them, and no one will ask . . .

"Ida, since your friend gave us a one-liner of good news, how about if you balance off with the bad. Ida?"

Ida stared at the semipermeable membrane and then at sick Eilene. The bad news was that she and Rose had found the group. "The good news is that I'm having a baby; the bad news is that I'm having a baby. In the morning, it's fantastic, but at night I feel horror."

"Why horror? Perhaps that word's a tiny bit strong." The instructor leaned on her other arm and noisily changed position. "Pardon me, my foot's gone to sleep. Go on, Ida."

"You're right. Horror is a ten o'clock word. At eight o'clock it feels like sadness."

Elwin's mother was resting against her husband's knees while he massaged the back of her neck. "Terror is the thought of an entire human being trying to fit through there, tearing his way through my most private part. I'll tell you, a C-section sounds better—*anything* sounds better."

The instructor explained that this fear was culturally conditioned, that many women feel only discomfort, not pain, that giving birth can be one of the most exhilarating experiences in a woman's life.

Suzi patted her stomach as though dribbling a basketball. "I pray that you're right, Lil, but listen, if each couple could decide who would have to do it," she drew a circle on the floor with her finger and put her thumb in the center of it, "here is a magic button, you each have one, okay? Push it and *he* has the exhilarating experience. Choose, right now, fast. Wouldn't you press it? Let's say it's anonymous, nobody knows how you vote—or even better, just an accident of fate, like having a girl or a boy, but really you've got this secret button and you can pick him or you. Choose."

"If it were before, I'd pick him. Afterwards, I'd probably choose me," said Joan.

"Something you want to be past already isn't something you're looking forward to."

Rose rocked forward with her weight on both hands. "Is that your terror, Ida?"

"No, at least not yet." To Suzi, "I'm not that far along."

In the car, on the way home, Ida sat up front next to Rose. Neither spoke until they crossed Commonwealth Avenue. Rose cleared her throat. "So, my love, tell me, was it such a bad idea, this childbirth class?"

Ida shrugged.

Rose checked her watch. "It's half-past sadness. You want to talk about it?"

From the B.U. bridge the water looked like black coffee. "Cream and sugar?"

"What?"

"Sorry. Sure I do. Rose, don't take it wrong. This is no reflection on you. But it's so fractured, my life. Fragmented. My husband—he still is, you know—is not the man I get to have children with, and the father, whom I love, won't even be there for the birth, and let's assume I marry again, it's still a third person to help me raise the child. And I don't want to dilute you and me, either. Both of us are the real parents."

"At least you've got good pieces. A good puzzle is better than a bad painting, no?" Rose parked in front of the house.

"I don't regret it, Rose. Don't get me wrong. The baby is *worth* it, but I still get to curse the inflation, don't I? Why am I charged more than everyone else!"

Rose started the car again. "How about Baskin and Robbins? A sundae with Heavenly Hash?"

"You're on."

They turned left at Central Square. "Ida, I forgot to ask you. What did you finally do about that cheating incident, with the letter to the father?"

"I ate it."

"What if someone asks?"

"They won't. Melanie won't ask, for fear it's simply been misplaced. She wouldn't want that error corrected. The administration will never suspect it didn't arrive, and the father doesn't know anything ever happened."

"And if anyone does find out, somehow?"

"A mistake. I forgot to mail it. Or better yet, I did send it out, so I thought. Lost in the mail."

There was a free space in front of the ice cream parlor. "Then you never really had to confront the thing, openly, and take responsibility for it."

"I did—through my actions, not my words."

Rose began to parallel park.

"Hey, today in class I taught some of Leonardo da Vinci's work. Did you know da Vinci had two mothers, sort of? The illegitimate one who kept him at first and then the woman his father married. Freud thought that's why he painted those overlapping maternal figures with the baby Jesus, like in *The Virgin and Saint Anne*."

"A perfect formula for genius, Ida. Works every time."

"Michelangelo, too. He was nursed for two years by a stonecutter's wife before his real mother took him back."

Rose turned around to lock the back door. "So with all the divorce and remarriage these days, why aren't we getting more Sistine Ceilings?"

14

"I bought you an Easter egg."

"But it isn't Easter yet."

"It should be. The Last Supper was a Passover *seder*, and that's tomorrow night."

The wind off the Charles smelled like grass-stained overalls. Phil began to peel the colored tinsel off the egg. "No bunny brought this one, Ida. It's big enough to be an ostrich egg."

"Well, that just goes to show there are some serious disadvantages to having a celibate clergy. First they tell you Mary was a virgin, and then they think that rabbits lay eggs. You need someone in there who knows what's what." Ida lay back in the sun on the warm grass.

"Old Dionysian fertility symbols. The spring festival. At least we remembered the birth bit. What kind of sex symbol is unleavened bread?"

"We have eggs, too. No sugar, though. Hard-boiled, and we dip them in salt water."

"That figures."

Ida noticed the chocolate tremble in his hands. "Oh, Phil."

"I guess the only ecumenical thing to do is cry on it."

Phil unwrapped the ace bandage and rewound it around his ankle.

"How's Marge?" Turning onto her side, Ida squeezed a

blade of grass between her fingers. She held it at the bottom and pulled upward, as hard as she could without it coming out of the ground.

"She's fine."

The grass made a high-pitched sound like washed hair when it's wet. "I've wanted to talk with you so often, Phil. But everything seems to have speeded up. First there was your conference, and then your leg, and then Marge up here to take care of you."

"Ida, I know I haven't been . . . It's the painkillers, too. I couldn't seem to get a grip on the papers I needed to correct, and the lectures I had to give on social movements crept up on me."

Creep, Ida thought. Crept.

He rolled a piece of the tinfoil into a ball half the size of his thumbnail.

Ida picked the strip of grass. "The baby kicked yesterday." She tried to tear the grass down the middle along the raised line.

"I wish I could have been there to feel it." Another piece of tinsel and a second ball.

"You couldn't have. It was just a little ripple on the inside, more of a touch than a kick. But still, it's a pretty strong baby. Guess it knocked you off your feet way before I even felt it."

"That's crazy, Ida. If it hadn't been for the accident . . ."

"If it hadn't been for the baby, you mean. Maybe you wouldn't have had the accident if it weren't for the baby."

Phil threw the tinsel balls toward the river, one at a time. "What are you saying, Ida? That the baby was an accident?"

"No. That your accident . . . I mean, there was nothing even there to trip on!"

"It happens, sometimes. You just put your weight down wrong. Honey, please, spare me the psychological crap. I've had enough trouble with the cast and the bindings and being laid up. Let's not blame the victim for a change, if that's all right."

Ida rested one hand on the lower hemisphere of her abdomen. "If my grandmother had wheels, she'd be a trolley car."

"What?"

"Nothing, forget it. Just something my mother-in-law used to say."

"You want some more chocolate?"

Ida shook her head. "No thanks. Phil, you can't let me in any more. I see that. Do you know what I'm saying? It's just that it all fell apart so suddenly! One minute you were there, and then you were gone." The grass wouldn't split neatly along the seam. Ida made a string of half moon cuts with her fingernail.

He threw the tinsel with his left hand, as though pitching. "I used to be ambidextrous."

"And now you can't even use both legs."

"Ida, cut it out! Anyway, it's two hearts that's the problem. I'm only one person—I have only one. With Marge up here, so close, I just couldn't . . ." He stared at his hands, one lying on the back of the other. Still. Only the second hand on his watch was moving. Not steadily; stopping and starting with each beat. Two forty-five. "I have a doctor's appointment at three. Marge is picking me up at school. I've got to head back."

Ida took the last piece of chocolate he'd been unpeeling.

"Okay. But it's funny. I've got just what I needed you to have: two hearts. Right inside me—somebody else's heart! Think of it. Maybe the baby's heart will help make up for the ones I've lost." Ida sat up slowly. "I'm feeling nauseous. I thought that part was mostly over by now."

"It's all this sugar you're eating. My Easter egg. I guess I should have brought *you* those real Easter eggs, the Jewish kind with the salt."

"Passover, not Easter. Freedom, not resurrection. We have more modest expectations." After picking up the last bits of foil wrapping, Ida put the clips back in Phil's ace bandage. "Too tight?"

"No. It's better that way. The less circulation, the less pain."

They walked along the river. "I want to put your name on the birth certificate. Do you think that's right?"

"Yes."

"Are you sure?"

"Yes. I told Marge about the child."

"I asked Rob to file for a divorce."

And Marge had hired a mover to help her pack for Phil because the doctor had forbidden any strain on the leg. With a proctor to give the final exams, he could leave for the West Coast two weeks early. Phil and Ida would write but not phone.

"If it's a boy, would you want to name him after me?"

"Certainly not. We only name children after the dead." Ida held him loosely around the waist, and he leaned on her shoulder with each step.

"Not after the lame?" With his free hand he touched her stomach.

"Not even for the blind or the mentally incompetent."

"Thanks a lot!" He pulled her closer and balanced on his good leg. "Ida, if only—"

"Sh, I can't stand to hear it. It's too late." She steadied her voice. "And anyway, no one should have someone else's name."

Ida sat in the car out front. A smear of pink was seeping through the gray sky. Solid, cloudless, the color of stainless steel. She'd gotten a late start and run into heavy traffic on the Mass. Pike. It had taken an extra hour to reach Manchester.

They probably started already. Past the four questions, even. "Why is this night different from all other nights?" If only it weren't at night! The tired, teary evenings. Ida usually chanted the *Kiddush* over the wine, since she had the best voice in the family. Uncle Norman couldn't sing at all. There would be an empty seat for her at the far end of the table, between her mother and Pearl. Maybe she could slip in quietly, smile, not disturb the service. Not have to talk to anybody.

Gracie's house was white with black shutters. Since they got the aluminum siding, the surface never aged. Always perfect. Bloated shrubs all around were the same dark green they painted swings with to keep them from rusting. Even on the front porch, the smell of soup.

No need to ring the doorbell and disrupt the *seder*. *Seder*, meaning order. Ida's translating reflex as she tried to keep the storm door from squeaking on its hinges. "I'm out of order," she thought. "Out of order, motion denied."

They had finished the song detailing the order of the service, Ida's *Kiddush*, and the dipping of green vegetables in salt water. They had finished the questions and started the answers. Uncle Norman was reading, ". . . they sat all night in B'nai Brak telling the story of the departure from

Egypt . . ." When Pearl saw Ida, she looked down at her cloth napkin, nodded, and then pointed to the baby's bottle. She left the dining room to check on little Arthur. Norman's voice went up and down. "Rabbi Elazar, the son of Azariah, said: Here I am a man of seventy years, yet I did not understand why the story of the departure from Egypt should be told at night." Ida slid in next to Mildred who was following along stiffly, running her finger down the margin of the page in the bright, new *haggadah* she had bought this year. Mildred wore dark glasses. "The days of your life might mean only the days, *all* the days of your life includes the nights also. Other sages explain it this way . . ."

Ida remembered Pearl's voice on the phone the night before. "Let me explain it this way, Ida. Now don't get me wrong, I'm not saying that Mother has any right to run your life for you, but neither do you have the right to shove it down her throat." Ida looked to the side at Mildred glued to her book. The skin around her mother's neck hung loosely at the front, vibrating as she read. Like old Mrs. Thelps at the Mary Cheney Library. "You can't imagine how upset she is. She's just not ready to handle it with the family yet. In the end, I'm sure she'll come around, after the baby is born and all, but this just isn't the right time." There were orange Creamsicles in her sister's voice. Ida, this just isn't *the right time*! Mother wanted us to *save* the Good Humor pops till after dinner. "This year it would probably be better if you didn't come home for Passover, especially since she's as much as told you so. It would be a deliberate slap in the face, if you know what I mean."

Norman glanced up. "Oh look, Ida's here. Just in time for *Baruch hamakom*. You lead us, Ida." Ida cleared her throat and started too low, but by the time she reached *l'amo Yisrael* it was within everyone's range. "Wonderful, Ida. Now let's go around and take turns reading. Grace?"

Aunt Grace sat between Norman and her elder son Nathan. "Blessit eeze God, who gave de Torah to Heeze people Eezrael. Blessit eeze He. De Torah speaks about four sons: one who eeze wise ahnd one who eeze contrary, one who eeze seemple, and one who does not even know how to ahsk a question." Grace spoke on a single pitch, enunciating each word as though chiseled in marble. When Ida was small, she had thought that Gracie was the only person who spoke English properly. "De contrary son ahsks: what eeze de meaning of theeze service to you? Saying *you*, he excludes heemself." Norman always said of Gracie, if she invites you to dinner, you either accept or move out of town.

So why am I doing this? Ida turned the pages quickly as Uncle Norman skipped ahead to the ten plagues so that the turkey in the oven wouldn't get overdone. "Blood, Fire, Pillars of Smoke . . ." Ida dipped her finger in her wine glass, dripping the excess onto the saucer to diminish her cup in memory of the punished Egyptians. Why did I come? To humiliate her, as Pearl thinks? Old obstinate Ida, that's probably what they think. To get it over with? To pretend to be strong, convincing myself by fooling others? "Locusts, Darkness, the Slaying of the First-Born." A flutter near her navel, just below the surface it seemed. For three days now, the tickle of new life. Ida put her hands down on her stomach. Orna, can you hear the singing from in there?

Nathan always read *Dayenu* after everyone sang it.

> Had He brought us out of Egypt and not executed judgment against them, *Dayenu*—it would have been enough for us.

Still time to back out, Ida thought. No need to mention it. Who knew? Had her mother spoken to Gracie?

> Had He divided the sea for us and not brought us through dry-shod, *Dayenu*—it would have been enough for us.

Should she talk to everyone individually or make some kind of announcement? This public service broadcast has been brought to you by . . .

"Dai dai yenu, dai dai yenu . . ." "Dayenu," thought Ida, "the national anthem of low expectations." Happy with half a cup.

Norman stood to demonstrate the Hillel sandwich, as he did every year. "Now put the herbs between the matza." He always pronounced *herbs* with an h. "Wait for the apple stuff to sweeten it. Gracie, where is it? Okay, this is the bread that didn't have a chance to rise when our ancestors left Egypt. The sweetness of freedom and the bitterness of slavery. Now for the meal!"

"No, Norman, first the eggs. Pass around the eggs and salt water."

Gracie was motioning to Ida. "Ida, dear, I hahve some fruit compote I need to take from de refreegerator een de basement. Come, you help me." Ida followed, relieved from having to speak to her mother. As soon as she came up, she could help serve the fish.

"Too bahd you were late, Ida dear. Leettle Deeky ahsked de four questions. Adorable, dat boy. One more year he'll do eet, and den Artie. Ach, a beauteeful baby." The stairway was dark, paneled in knotty pine, and at the bottom the checkerboard linoleum where Ida and Pearl had played hopscotch with Nathan. Masking tape for lines. Step on a crack, break your mother's back. "And den anodder year or two for Artie, and den yours."

Ida froze. With the glass bowl of cooked fruit she had been handed.

Gracie turned around with the second tureen. "Yes, your modder told me. Now, I know what Vera will say, and de odders, but I want you to know one ting. Here—deeze eeze heavy. Put eet down on de stairs. You know my Natan was born in de D.P. cahmp, ahfter de war. You know dat. Well, people said eet was wrong, een a cahmp. What future deed we hahve, to know for sure? Nutting, we hahd den. And Normahn and I, when could I come bahck weed heem to de States, weed my soldier? Who knew? But we hahd to stahrt. You hahve to stahrt. I know."

Ida was crinkling the edge of the cellophane that covered the compote. "Oh, Aunt Grace . . ."

"No, you don't need to say nutting. Save eet for de odders. We go up now. I just wanted you to hear deeze from me, first." Ida's face was hot against her aunt's cool hand, which smelled like the dishcloth. Wide weave, white with blue stripes, soaked in Ivory liquid. "About your modder, don't worry so much. I know my cousin. I work on her."

"Gracie, that was the best sponge cake you ever made. Light as a cloud. Couldn't even tell it was made from matza meal." Vera piled the dessert plates she'd gathered onto the kitchen counter. "So, Ida, how is Boston treating you?"

"While you're gahbbing, maybe you could shake out de tableclot for me, yes? Den put eet bahck on before we stahrt de rest of de serveece."

Ida and Vera rolled up the linen to keep the crumbs from dropping on the rug. "Isn't that Artie something? Not quite a year and he's practically standing on his own! I swear, he has my brother's eyes." Vera kicked the back door open for Ida. "My dear, you've put on a little weight, I think. All that Boston cream pie, right?" Vera held one end of the tablecloth and Ida the other. "Perhaps we shouldn't put this back on the table, with that wine spill."

Ida folded her end. "Vera, I guess this is as good a time as any. It's not fat. I'm pregnant."

Vera looked at her niece as though Ida had just confessed to a murder. Vera covered her open mouth with her hand.

In Vera's skeletal stare, Ida caught the echo of a painting by Edvard Munch. *The Scream*. In black and white, like a print in the textbook *Arts and Ideas*. Ida let a laugh trickle out. "Take it easy, Auntie Veer, from this you don't die."

"Oh, Ida, darling, I'm so sorry . . ."

"I'm not." Ida explained that she wanted the baby.

"And Rob still wants a divorce, I mean, but I thought . . ."

"No, Vera, Rob's not the father." Ida hesitated. "There are ways today."

"Oh. Oh yes! Your mother told me about your friend, Rose, who lost the baby. But I never thought . . . Your mother never. Ah! And Mildred said she had conjunctivitis! The dark glasses—we never thought to . . . we . . . Ida, who else knows? Why wasn't I told!"

"You just were, Vera. Come on in. Gracie knows, that's all. We'll tell the rest after they finish the *seder*. It's no secret."

"*Shir Hamaalot* . . ." "A song of ascent," Ida translated to herself. Although Norman was leading the grace in a loud voice, the two sides of the table were singing at different speeds. Pearl and Paul had already left because the baby was getting cranky, Uncle Alex was talking to Morty about the Giants' winning streak, and Mildred was removing pieces of matza that Artie had dropped behind the cushion of the wing chair.

"Not very good, folks," Norman scolded. "That wasn't supposed to be a round. All right, we'll skip *Key Lo Naeh*. Alex, shut up and do the fourth cup of wine."

"Blessed art Thou, Eternal our God . . ."

Ida read on ahead. "*Chasal sidur Pesach k'hilchato.*" Ended is the Passover *seder* according to its way. "*K'chal mishpato v'chukato,*" sang the others. According to its judgment and laws.

"Don't believe it for a minute," said Norman, flipping through the pages that remained. "Far from finished. 'Next year in Jerusalem,' everybody. This time let's try to sing on key."

Adir Hu was a disaster. The song was much too high. "Okay, this next one we're good at. More questions. Everybody takes a part. Gracie, you be number one, Nathan you're two, Morty you're three, and so on around the table. Alex, pay attention. Now, 'Who knows the meaning of number one?' " Round and round the table: ". . . eleven are the stars in Joseph's dream, ten are the commandments, nine are the months of childbirth, eight are the days before circumcision, seven are the days of the week, six are the sections of the Mishnah, five are the books of the Torah, four are the matriarchs, three are the patriarchs, two are the tablets of the covenant . . ."

"And a partridge in a pear tree," thought Ida.

Chad Gadya. Ida sang with the others. "The angel of death that killed the butcher that slaughtered the ox that drank the water that quenched the fire that burned the stick that beat the dog that bit the cat that ate the goat my father bought . . ."

"One little goat, one little goat." Ida pictured yellow stretch suits and bubble bibs. Hey diddle diddle, the cat and the fiddle, the cow jumped over the moon. "Next year in Jerusalem." At Menachem's wall. Next year, little Orna. Next year.